Blood Trail

John Harvey is a prolif[illegible]ers and westerns; he also writes, edits and publish[illegible]y. At present he is doing research and a little teaching in th[illegible] American Studies department of Nottingham University. He likes going to movies and a few other things.

In the same series:

Hart One:
Cherokee Outlet

Hart Three:
Tago

Hart Four:
The Silver Lie

John B. Harvey

Hart Two:
Blood Trail

Pan Original
Pan Books London and Sydney

First published 1980 by Pan Books Ltd,
Cavaye Place, London SW10 9PG

ISBN 0 330 25993 8
Set, printed and bound in Great Britain by
Cox & Wyman Ltd, Reading

to the memory of
James M. Cain
1892–1977

One

The wind moved westward across the grass, bending it in swathes. An endless expanse of high plain that swerved like a green sea. The sky that covered it was steel grey; the blue-tinged grey of gun metal. If a man looked to the east, into the eye of the wind, he could see a dull, jagged line of yellow that cracked across the greyness like a bowl someone had dropped carelessly.

A man looked.

Wes Hart leaned back in the saddle and turned his head in the direction he'd come. Three days he'd been riding; three days since he'd flung his deputy's badge in the marshal's face; three nights since he'd faced Charlie Bowdre and Dan Halloran across a camp-fire and put two slugs into Halloran that had left him for dead, breast bone smashed apart.

Riding west the way he'd come, Hart had seen scarcely a living soul – unless you counted jack rabbits and white-tailed deer and such. Once, between Red Fork and Deep Fork in the Creek Nation, a bunch of Indians had followed him for three or four miles, just trailing after him, never getting any nearer. Likely wondering whether it was worth the risk of riding in under his guns and trying to get his handsome dapple grey mare away from him. If that had been the case, they'd thought better of it. As suddenly as they'd appeared they'd slipped away again.

Within sight of the Cimarron he'd met up with an old timer trading goods out of his wagon. Aside from the Indian agencies and the forts, he'd be lucky to find a customer from one month's end to the next.

Hart had bought a piece of dried salt beef from him, along with a small sack of coffee. The old man had been glad of the trade, glad of the company. For the best part of half an hour Hart had listened to him rambling on about every damn thing that teemed into his head. His one remaining tooth had showed clearly at the right of his mouth and a thin line of almost white slaver had run down from both corners. Only once had he really pricked Hart's attention.

A band of Cheyenne had ridden north east and crossed the Cimarron less than a week back. A raiding party, twenty or more braves.

The old timer must have recognized Hart's quickened interest, for he chuckled and rubbed more vigorously at the dark tobacco in the palm of his hand.

'They after horses,' Hart had asked, 'or ridin' some kind of grudge?'

The old man shook his head and pushed some of the tobacco into the corner of his mouth. 'Never seen 'em. Only heard.'

'Heard what?' Hart's voice had edged harder.

'Attacked a few settlements, run off some stock, Lord knows there ain't much in this damned country worth fightin' for.'

'You know any places? Names?'

The old man spat a squirt of rich brown juice down into the grass and a length of it hung for several moments before falling.

'Got friends up that ways? Folk?'

Hart had shaken his head and stood up; it wasn't any use questioning him any closer. There was only one way to find out and that was to see for himself. He'd left the old man messing with the harness of his mules and shaking his head at younger men's impatience.

Letting the grey move into a trot Hart thought back to what the man had said about friends and folk. A wry smile played at the even line of his mouth. He had kin somewhere: a brother and three sisters. Last time he'd seen any of them was over twenty years back. The girls in a line, patched aprons tied about them, white faces staring up at him as he sat bareback on the old plough horse. The youngest, Christine, biting her lip and trying not to let the tears come. Ann and Veronica simply staring, not understanding. Sean, three years of age, held fast to the fence post and refused to look at Wes at all.

Hart couldn't remember what he'd said, what any of the girls had said. He just saw them all frozen in that moment, like in a daguerreotype.

Eighteen fifty-eight. He'd been fourteen. Now he was thirty-five. Thirty-five and when the old man had asked if he had friends he couldn't answer.

Hell! What did it matter?

Hart touched the grey with his spurs and the mare responded, stretching her legs beneath him.

He rode tall in the saddle, the wind tugging at the sleeves of the dark green wool shirt that he wore. A flat-crowned black hat was held on his head by a loop of narrow cord. Brown pants were tucked into boots of scuffed, plain leather. None of these things marked him out as anything different from most other men who might be riding across the territory.

What did were the weapons he carried. The handgun that sat in a cutaway holster was a Colt Peacemaker .45 with a mother-of-pearl grip upon which was carved the likenesses of an eagle and a snake; the eagle grasped the snake in its beak and with both claws.

Two more guns were sheathed on either side of his saddle. On the left there was a lever-action Henry .44 rifle with a fitted rear sight. On the right something more curious. A Remington 10-gauge shotgun, its twenty-eight-inch barrels sawn down to little over half their normal length.

A double-bladed knife was hanging in an Apache sheath that was tied to the pommel of his saddle. A second pistol, a double-action Starr .44, was out of sight in the saddle bags that were partly covered by his blue, red and white Indian blanket.

His weapons and his eyes: from up close, his eyes.

From his lean, stubbled face with its high, prominent cheek-bones and from under the brim of his hat and the falling wisp of darkening brown hair, they stared out at the world. Seeing everything, registering but rarely showing feeling. At times those faded blue eyes burnt with the strength of cold fire.

Hart reined in and stood in his stirrups. The dark blotch ahead to the left would be Guthrie, at the edge of the Cimarron where the river bent southwards. He could ride in there and get a meal, a drink, take a bath while his horse was tended to. Or he could cross the river and go on to Stillwater straight.

He remembered the single tooth waggling in the old timer's head and heard again his words about the Cheyenne. Hart looked up at the sky and it was still steel grey.

'C'mon, Clay.'

He flicked and pulled at the reins and headed towards the Cimarron. The water was cold and surged against his legs, splashing up into his chest and back. Hart kept his mount under tight control, fighting the current. His gun belt bounced against him from where he had fastened it about his neck.

When the mare pushed through and clambered up the far bank, both man and animal shook themselves free of excess water and were eager to move into a gallop.

Soon the only traces of dampness on the horse's neck were of sweat.

Stillwater was stranded in the middle of the plain like the whitening skeleton of a buffalo the hunters had stripped bare and left. Once it had been a stage depot on the route south from Wichita, but the line had transferred west to Baker's Stage Station and most of the point had been drained from Stillwater's existence.

The old depot, low and long with its reinforced log walls, was the only building of any substance left. The few stores that had grown up there were mostly abandoned except to the wind. There were a handful of cabins and a few more sod houses and that was it.

Stillwater.

Hart brought his horse to a standstill and shifted the angle of his hat on his head. He expected the place to look pretty dead, but . . .

Automatically his right hand went to the butt of his Colt, lifting it a little inside the polished and greased holster and letting it fall back. His left hand reached for the stock of the Henry and pulled it out of the scabbard. Moving the rifle across his body, he levered a shell into the chamber.

'Clay.'

The animal's name came out as a whisper and Hart rocked his body in the saddle. The grey went forwards at a slow walk,

Hart's eyes moving from side to side, eating in every detail.

The first thing he saw was a leg, a man's leg in dark blue pants pushing its way through the open doorway of one of the sod houses. There was no need for Hart to dismount – he could read enough into the leg's angle and its obvious stiffness.

Next it was a bright flutter of yellow, a piece of cotton material flapping in the east wind. Hart swung his right leg over the saddle and dropped silently to the ground. Rifle angled across his chest, finger tight against the trigger, he went forward.

The material was part of a dress; the yellow was traced through with the faint pattern of flowers; it blew against the side of the wooden frame door and then rested back on the bare skin of the woman's leg. As Hart watched the wind continued to move it, as if it had life.

Hart eased the door back with his boot. The interior of the soddie was dark and smelt of damp and something else. Damp and dried blood and something else. He dropped into a crouch beside the woman's body.

A knife wound cut deep across her chest, slicing through the top of her yellow dress and the woollen garment she had been wearing underneath. It sliced through her left breast, folding the heavy, pendulous flesh on either side of a wound that was now ridged with scabbed blood.

It had not killed her. What had killed her was a blow to the side of the head with something blunt, heavy, a war club. There was just enough of the top of the head remaining to tell. Whoever had taken the woman's scalp had done so in a hurry. The skin below the knife incision had ripped badly, coming loose almost to the bridge of her nose. The bared roof of her skull was matted with dark blood and thick with the almost silent movement of small insects.

Hart turned his head aside and stood up. Outside in the air he breathed deeply and moved on.

The crack in the sky had disappeared; the greyness had thickened and was pressing down, closing. The wind had finally wrenched the sign away from its one remaining nail above what had been the saddler's. The square of painted wood bounced and slid across open ground, stopping against the broken-down fence of the stable.

Hart kicked back a warped door and went inside. There was a fast scuttle away from the centre of the room and something moving low and close to the ground. Hart brought the Henry to chest height and fired once, twice, three times. The sound of the rifle echoed round the almost empty room; light from doorway and window showed up the outlines of a cupboard, two chairs, a bed whose mattress had been pulled towards the floor. The straw stuffing had been ripped out in several places, and spilled out of the gaps savaged in its striped cover. Lying close by the bed, close to the room's centre were two children. It was hard to tell, but from their size they were likely around six or seven.

The picture of Hart's youngest sister, Christine, standing and biting her lip as he prepared to ride away, jumped unbidden to his mind.

Hart shook his head as if physically to clear the image away. He looked from the mattress to the children's faces to the dark, bloodied bodies of rats he had shot in the corner of the room. Vomit rose to the back of his throat and he choked it back down.

He slammed the door behind him and walked to the old depot building, striding fast. Curving trails of flour wound their way from the entrance; a sack had been dropped and left in the haste of their going. Rats had been at that, too. A bolt of bright blue cloth unravelled itself through one of the side windows and the wind tangled it tighter and tighter.

Hart stepped over the dead man who lay immediately inside the doorway and went inside. The tin chimney from atop the central stove had been smashed down and lay in sections. Tables had been upturned to use as shields. In one of them a group of three arrows stuck as close and tight as a man's heart.

Broken glass was scattered all over the long room, here and there dark with dried blood.

One man had tried to get out through a window. He must have been almost through when the axe head had been driven into his spine. The wound ploughed deep; the white of bone showed through, smeared and stained.

Amos Grant sat in the same armchair he always took his rest in. Arrows pinned him to it, fixed fast through his body – arms and side, one piercing the folds of his belly, another through his neck, the hardwood shaft narrowly missing the windpipe.

Grant's fingers gripped the frayed fabric of the chair arms, almost as if he were sitting there waiting for the barber to step across to the depot and give him his weekly shave and maybe trim the thinning wisps of hair that fell past his ears.

Hart wondered why they hadn't scalped him, as they had most of the others.

He wondered what had happened to the old Colt Navy Grant had used to back him up not too many weeks before.

He wondered what the old man had thought as he died; if he had thought anything at all.

Hart remembered sitting by the stove with him, a bottle of good whisky passing to and fro between the pair of them. As the night had worn on, Grant's eyes had become misted as he'd moved further and further back in time. He'd told Hart of his wife, Sophie, how the two of them had bundled all their belongings on to a wagon and joined a train heading west. Smiling in their hopes for a new life. She'd never lasted those last years and Amos Grant had been glad.

In the end all he'd had left were his old gun and the horse-hair armchair and a few memories which betrayed him whenever they strayed into his mind.

Hart leaned forward and touched the man's cheek: it was cold, waxen, the flesh beneath it set hard. Hart tightened the line of his mouth and stepped away. It took him a quarter of an hour to find what he was looking for. He drank a third of the bottle of whisky first and then he went out with the spade and dug a deep, wide hole through the sod and dark earth.

It wasn't easy shifting man and chair out together but he managed it. He cut away the arrows at the level of the body and threw them into the wind. Then he lowered the chair down into the grave, Amos Grant sliding over to one side as he went down. Hart drank some more of the whisky before filling the grave in. By the time he'd finished sweat was pouring from his arms and down his back, making the wool of his shirt stick to his skin. The sides of his brown hair were flat and wet against his temples. Muscles in his arms ached.

Finally he fetched the saddler's sign and scratched Grant's name on to the back of it with the point of his knife. He hammered the board into the head of the grave with the flat of the shovel.

Hart stood straight and stretched his arms and back. He picked up the whisky bottle and raised it over the mound of newly turned earth.

'Here's to you, Amos.'

He set the lip of the bottle to his mouth and swallowed hard; the raw liquor burned the back of his throat. He moved his arm and upturned the bottle, letting the remains of the whisky splash down over the grave.

Then he hurled the bottle against the wall of the depot and let the smash of glass shatter the silence.

The stink of death clung to the inside of Wes Hart's head; the touch of it to his fingers. He hated it, feared it, refused to think about it. As soon as a man who lived by the gun thought too long about death it claimed him, slowing his hand when he made his draw, making him careless about walking into darkened alleys, about sitting with his back to the street.

He climbed up into the saddle and urged the mare through the town, towards the greying horizon. Already the sign at the head of Amos Grant's grave had tilted towards the ground.

Two

Hart's direction was due south, towards the Cimarron. The day was closing in about him as he rode, the wind driving into him, stronger than before. He reached round behind and loosed the knots that held the blanket in place. Twisting the reins round the saddle pommel, he threw the blanket round his body so that it hung over his right shoulder with a loose knot below his left hip.

He'd had the blanket the best part of ten years, since scouting for the army amongst the Navajo. He'd got himself working under a captain called Rodway who reckoned he knew everything in the whole damned world that'd been invented and quite a few things that hadn't. Sure claimed to be an expert on Indians – so expert he thought it was his right to wipe them out of existence.

It wasn't that he bore them any grudge; on the contrary, Rodway had a lot more respect for the Indian than most whites, especially those in the army. He simply thought they were in the way.

'The Indian is a primitive,' he'd say, holding forth to his fellow officers, 'even one with signs of some kind of civilization like the Navajo. He has no ambition to rise beyond his gods or do more than grow corn for his family and weave blankets. This country needs land to grow and the Indian simply sits in the way.'

Hart remembered him: thin, bow-legged, body like a greyhound; dark hair flattened to his scalp, intense dark eyes that were rarely still, a beaked nose over thin, small lips.

'I've got nothing against the Indian,' he said, 'I simply see it as my duty to eliminate him.'

Hart hadn't seen it that way. At first he'd tried to argue, but the position of most scouts around an army troop was like that of a dog round a camp fire. When Rodway wouldn't listen, Hart had tried stronger methods; the captain had him clapped in the guardhouse. Hart had broken out and ridden off to warn the Navajo.

He Who Runs had presented him with his own chief's blanket

in thanks. Three days later the Indian had been cut down by the sabre of a charging cavalry man and had died after another two days of great pain.

Hart had always kept the blanket with him; it kept him warm and it reminded him of a people he'd learned to respect. If it came to a choice between their civilization and that which produced men like Rodway, he was pretty certain where his allegiance would be.

Now he pushed his hat back on his head and felt the wind tug at his hair. The line of trees he recognized was less than a mile off. He spoke to the grey mare and touched her sides with his spurs, moving her into a canter. Soon the valley began to form to his left and Hart rode along the top of the ridge, looking for the cabin.

Some feeling gnawed at his insides, something that was close to fear yet was different. It had to do with someone other than himself and he couldn't pin it down. Maybe he didn't want to. He'd only seen her twice; spoken to her once. Carol. Carol Peterson. The first time she'd stepped out into strong sunlight and her fair hair had glowed like fine gold. Only closer had he seen the life in her green eyes – life and knowledge of life. At the back of the vivacity a knowledge of sorrow.

He'd stopped for less than half an hour, taken the coffee and sourdough biscuits she'd given him, all the while watching her, watching her and pretending not to.

Next time he'd ridden by she'd been out front of the place again only she'd been with her husband. Hart hadn't bothered to stop, simply rode on.

So what was he expecting now? Why had he ridden out the way he had? Hart shook his head and slowed the mare to a walk. First time that trader had mentioned the Cheyenne he'd thought of her; thought of the feeling that batch of pine close to the back of their cabin had given him. When he'd knelt alongside the woman back in Stillwater, the one with the yellow dress, it had been Carol that he'd been thinking of, fearing for.

And now?

There was no figure outside the building; even in the thickening darkness he would have picked out her hair. The cabin seemed unreal; the barn to its left almost finished, a small corral in front of that which was empty. No smoke rose up from the chimney.

Those pines, they were too close, gave too much cover for anyone who wanted to . . .

Hart pushed his tongue against the inside of his cheek and reached his right hand to his Colt .45, testing its weight and balance as it slid from the holster. He spun the chamber across his left palm before dropping it back into place.

'Clay.'

The horse began to angle its way down the side of the valley, Hart alert to the slightest movement, the first sign of danger. Since he'd seen it last the remainder of the fresh wood of the building had been tarred, extra shutters of small, split logs fixed over the windows. The door, double thickness, was fastened close.

Hart slipped from the saddle and eased the Colt into his hand. In the silence the triple click of the hammer being worked back was oddly loud.

He walked around the cabin, searching for whatever signs he could make out. There were none: neither of attack nor anything else. It was as if no one lived there – had ever lived there.

The door was shut fast. Hart leaned his weight against it and it swung heavily back. The inside was dark and Hart went into it fast, moving the gun from left to right in an arc. No one, nothing moved.

The door grated on its hinges behind him.

Hart waited until his eyes became accustomed to the light then stepped over to the table and lifted the smoked glass from the body of a kerosene lamp. He struck a match on the end of his pistol butt and turned up the wick. Flame surged upwards with a sharp orange glow; Hart set the glass back in place and stood away.

Chairs, chest of drawers, stove; blue patterned plates, gold-rimmed cups, a picture of Carol in a carved wood frame – everything was set perfectly in place.

Hart went into the second room. The white cover had been smoothed down on the four-poster bed. Three pairs of boots, two larger than the third, were polished and standing next to one another under the shuttered window. Clothes hung neatly inside the wardrobe.

A thin film of dust had settled over everything.

When the door creaked again Hart went outside and unsaddled the mare, leading her into the barn. There was straw in one corner and an empty trough. He fetched water from the well at back of the house.

If it had been Cheyenne there would have been some sign. Maybe they'd been warned about the attack on Stillwater and cleared out fast? But that didn't explain nothing being taken with them; the orderliness of the place.

Hart set his saddle bags on the table and took a piece of dried beef and some biscuits from his supplies. There was a jar of coffee on one of the shelves close by the stove. He went outside and fetched wood. The sky was almost totally black now and only a few stars broke its cover. When he looked behind, the pines seemed close enough to touch.

He slid the bolt across the door and pushed the solid wooden bar into place; then he made certain the windows were secured. Only after that was done did he light the stove.

When the wood had caught and Hart was staring into the flickering flames he remembered those last moments before he'd turned in his badge. He could see, clear as if it were before him, the scaffold back at Fort Smith; see the kid he'd brought in for trial and the look on his face as he swung and choked, choked and swung. As the young neck had stretched, so his face had been sent sideways and his tongue forced from his mouth, purple and swollen; his eyes had bulged until Hart had thought they'd burst from their sockets. The harsh spluttered sounds of death coming slow and the stink of excrement. Finally, two men hanging on to his boots and jerking him down.

No: there wasn't anything you could do to a man that was worse than hanging him. Not even the treatment the Cheyenne had given back in Stillwater. At least their victims had a chance to run, to fight back. But hanging . . . Hart shook his head. Any killing he had to do, he'd do himself, face to face if possible. In his own way and with his own hands.

He went to take the coffee pot from the stove. Not much later he'd pulled back the covers on the Peterson's bed and stripped down to his long johns. The mattress was deep and soft and he was asleep almost as soon as his head settled into the white pillow.

He was aware of dreaming and at one stage there was a woman but she wasn't Carol Peterson.

Bird call woke him and as he stirred his hand moved towards his gun, hanging in the holster from one post of the bed. For a moment he was unsure where he was, but as that passed he let his fingers fall away from the Colt, pushed back the sheets and swung his legs round till his feet touched the floor. He stood up, yawned, wiped the rims of his eyes and pulled on his pants. He put on his shirt but left it unbuttoned.

Water from the well.

Hart slid the bars and bolts away from the door and stepped out into the early morning. The air hit him as a kind of shock; the increased light made him blink. To his right, away from the ridge, the sun was spreading orange-gold along the horizon. He went round the cabin and filled the wooden bucket, letting it splash over his arms as he carried it back.

Three feet short of the doorway a shell tore into the wood inches to his left. The sound of a rifle was clear in his head as he dropped the bucket and dived forwards. Head going under, shoulders dipping, he rolled through a somersault that sent his legs crashing into the table, knocking it askew across the room. A second shot had sounded as he was going forward, now a third – the shell ricocheted off the edge of the door jamb and angled through the room, smashing one of the patterned plates on the dresser.

Hart's own rifle was nearest.

He lunged for it, working the lever, bringing the stock up against his shoulder, sliding forward to the doorway.

The ridge was lit by the sun across the valley; trees were beginning to separate out. Hart scanned the line, faded blue eyes alert and taking in every detail. Nothing, no one moved.

He sprang outside and dropped low to his left, the Henry tracing the ridge from tree to tree. No. Yet Hart was positive that was where the shots had come from. He turned and ran to the barn, talking to Clay as soon as he entered, leading the mare out and catching hold of her mane to jump on to her back.

As he rode towards the hill he heard, beneath the sound of the mare's hoofs, another horse galloping away.

'C'mon!'

Hart leaned forward, stroking the dapple grey's neck and urging her up the slope. When he reached the ridge he slowed her down, walking her along the narrow track. After a few moments he dropped down and examined the ground.

Someone had been there, waiting, kneeling there for some little time. His horse had been tied on the far edge. When he'd ridden away it had been down the opposite diagonal to the one Hart had climbed.

The sun beyond the cabin had cleared the horizon and was strong and bright, blinding him. Someone had known he was there: it had to be. Or they had thought him someone else. But why wait and try and bushwack him like that, then ride off without getting the job done?

And who?

Hart turned his head and looked in the direction the would-be killer had taken.

Who?

Hart blinked back into the sun and climbed back on to the mare. When he'd shot Dan Halloran, Charlie Bowdre hadn't made a play. He'd told Hart he didn't intend to and Hart had believed him. Besides, trying to put a bullet through the back of his head wasn't Charlie's style – then again, Hart thought with a rueful smile, if Charlie had tried that, likely he wouldn't have missed.

He looked at the line of pale wood gouged out of the wall close by the door; at the chunk of thick wood driven away from the jamb. Inside the cabin shattered pieces of plate were strewn over the far side of the floor.

Hart pulled the table back into place and used the side of his boot to push the broken china into a heap. There was something unsettling about the way the almost anonymous neatness of the cabin had been threatened.

The questions continued to move through Hart's mind as he refilled the bucket from the well, washed in the bracing coldness of the water, boiled coffee on the stove. Had the bullets been meant for him and if so who wanted him dead?

Hart thought he'd ride across to Guthrie after all. He could stock up on supplies, get some more shells and maybe ask a few questions of a different kind. Now that he'd turned in his badge there was work to find – he had to let the news get out that he was for hire.

Waiting for the coffee to heat through, Hart stripped down his Colt and cleaned and oiled it thoroughly.

Three

Originally Guthrie had been so close to the southern bank of the Cimarron that every time the flood water had risen, the houses had got washed out. After a particularly bad rainy season in which the inhabitants had been forced to take to their roofs three times in as many weeks, they broke the places up and rebuilt them further back from the river.

The Cimarron itself had originally been crossed by a ferry, which the zealous citizens had replaced with a bridge when the stage line decided to come over at that point. One February morning the struts gave way and the stage went over with the wavering bridge, tossing four passengers, driver, guard and strong box into the river.

Since then the stage line had changed its route to cross further up river and a new ferry had been built at Guthrie. Wes Hart leaned on the side rail and gazed at the water lapping up around the end of the planking. Besides himself and his horse, the only other folk travelling were the ferryman and his assistant, who was pulling them over, hauling in on the rope that was slung across from one bank to the other.

'You ain't no lawman, are you?'

The ferryman was medium height, his left shoulder raised unnaturally high and slightly humped. A greyish beard and whiskers sprouted out from his face in no particular direction and he squinted at Hart through narrowed eyes.

Hart looked back at the man and shook his head.

'Outlaw?' The word was accompanied by a high chuckle.

Again the shake of the head.

'Thought you must be one or the other.'

'Don't nobody else use this ferry?'

The man turned sideways and jerked his body so that his hump pushed higher into the air. 'Sure,' he said. 'But they don't look like you.' He nodded towards Hart's saddle guns. 'Don't go armed that way.'

'Uh-huh.' Hart nodded and stepped along the ferry; the southern bank was fast approaching.

The ferryman came up close behind him and Hart's hand drifted towards the butt of his Colt.

'Goin' through or stayin'?'

Hart fixed him with a stare. 'Both.'

The man gazed up at him and chuckled, backing away as he did so, scratching at the side of his unruly beard.

The end of the ferry pushed aground and the assistant jumped on to the bank and tied it up. He was young, strongly muscled, brown hair cropped short. When he opened his mouth to speak only an unformed wordless tumble of sounds came out.

The ferryman pointed at him and looked at Hart. 'That's Jonah. His pa was a preacher. Hell fire an' brimstone. The boy here took to stealin' an' lyin' the way a fish takes to water. His pa tried to whip it outta him but didn't do no good. Fin'ly told one lie too many. Preacher man took up this sharp little knife and held that boy down across t'kitchen table an' sliced th' end of his tongue right off. That's been closest he can get to talkin' ever since.'

The ferryman chuckled: 'Stops him lyin' but he'll still steal th' clothes off your back if'n he gets the chance.'

The muscled youngster beamed up at Hart and jumped back on to the end of the ferry. Hart swung himself up into Clay's saddle and rode slowly on to the bank.

'Be seein' you,' the ferryman called. 'Maybe.'

Hart gave a quick, short wave of his hand without turning round and flicked at the rein so that the grey broke into a trot.

The first places he came to in Guthrie were of shaky frame construction with tarpaper roofs; after a while the buildings became more substantial, the roofs of planking or shingle. Hart nodded at a man who called up to him from the side of the street, just someone passing the time of day. And it was a better day than the one before – the wind still blew east by north-east, but it had slackened in force and lost its cutting edge. The sun which had been so strong early that morning had faded some as it had risen in the sky but still gave out warmth none the less.

Hart passed a saddlers on his right, a fine Texas saddle in the centre of the window, its pommel decorated with silver. Behind it, on either side, were a range of headstalls and bits – spade, ring, curb and half-breed. Next to that was a drug store with a sign that read *Hostetter's Bitters* hanging outside.

Hart noted the eating house and a couple of saloons and rode on up the street towards the livery stable. Two kids were outside the high-roofed barn washing down a rig and several other rigs stood off to one side. One of them, a boy with a mass of fair hair, stopped what he was doing and looked up at Hart, giving him a half-smile.

'Hi, mister.'

Hart turned away, hearing someone coming out of the barn.

'Got a good stall free.'

The man stood at the barn entrance, scraping dirt from the prongs of a hay fork with a piece of stick. He was tall and tending towards fat, his stomach lowering itself on to a broad leather belt and pushing through the rucks of his sweated shirt.

'Best feed for miles, assure you of that.'

Hart dropped to the ground. 'Only feed for miles, ain't it?'

The man put his head to one side and eyed Hart quizically but said nothing. Not straight off. A few moments later he was telling the fair-haired boy to leave what he was doing and see to the stranger's horse.

'Stayin' long?' the liveryman asked, still working at the hay fork.

'Couple of days.'

'Driftin' through, huh?'

'Sort of.'

The liveryman took half a pace back and appeared to be weighing Hart up.

'You, er, lookin' for work.'

'I ain't about to mess out no stables.'

'Didn't mean that. I was thinkin' more of that gun you're totin'.'

Hart's eyes narrowed as he returned the man's gaze keenly. 'Could be.'

The liveryman's mouth opened a little as if he was about to say more, but he changed his mind and closed it again. Hart figured it could wait; if the man knew anything worth knowing it would as likely come out later.

Again the liveryman seemed about to speak but thought better of it. Hart collected his weapons and saddle bags and walked back along the main street. The sign above the eating house announced that the only steak sold on the premises was prime and fresh, that the proprietor was a Mrs Eileen McMurty and that there were rooms for rent by the night or by the week.

Eileen McMurty was around sixty years old with a reddish wobble of loose skin about her neck that made her look like a turkey in lace and bombazine. She peered at Hart through steel-rimmed spectacles and demanded money in advance before he was even allowed to set his things down on the floor.

'No smoking in bed, no boots worn in bed and no lady visitors!'

'In bed?'

'In the room!'

Mrs McMurty shut the door with a fierce show of independent spirit and Hart grinned and began to unbutton his shirt, anxious to wash off the dirt of the trail. Twenty minutes later he was getting ample proof of the fact that whatever Mrs McMurty's faults might be, lying wasn't one of them. The steak that slipped off both ends of Hart's plate was as fresh and prime as he'd tasted.

Every few minutes she walked stiff-backed into the dining-room, skirts brushing the floor, and stared at the tables as if daring any of the customers to complain.

There were some half dozen others apart from Hart. A couple of ranch hands, a drummer in a pin-stripe suit, what looked to be a pair of newly-weds from the way they kept staring into one another's eyes and holding hands between bites, and a mulatto with a cast in his left eye and a way of sidling glances at everyone else that was close to unsettling.

Once Hart caught his expression and held it for a few seconds before the man looked away.

Hart finished his meal and ordered coffee. It was as well Mrs McMurty didn't say anything about her coffee outside; Hart might have tasted weaker, meaner coffee somewhere but he couldn't recall where. After a couple of mouthfuls, he pushed the cup away and left.

The first saloon he came to was the Deuce of Clubs and it stank like the leavings of a rabid goat – and that was in the day time.

The Guthrie Star was smaller but cleaner and the sawdust strewn over the floor looked fresh enough to have been put there that morning. Hart ordered a couple of beers and drank one off straight, taking the second to a table and sitting with it for a while.

In mid-swallow he realized that someone was looking at him and spotted the mulatto peering over the top of the bat-wing doors. Hart set his glass down slowly and by the time it had touched the table the man had gone.

Behind him three men argued about the merits of a particular brand of seed and a fourth man, by himself close to the window, snored with the ragged rise and fall of his breath.

The bartender polished glasses with the bottom of his striped apron, whistling a tune that Hart recognized but couldn't put a name to.

Soon Hart was ready to go and the second glass of beer drained. He was midway out of his chair when the doors swung back and a group of five men walked through, not too fast but with a sense of purpose.

'Mayor! You want the usual?'

The leader of the group glanced over towards the bar, shaking his head in a manner that suggested he was affronted. The bartender shrugged and let it go.

The mayor of Guthrie was portly and walked with a left leg that seemed to be stiff from the thigh down. He had a silver watch chain strung across his dark blue vest like it was a symbol of office. The couple on his right were also wearing suits fresh from the latest shipment into the local store; one had a neatly clipped moustache which seemed out of place on his florrid face, the second kept twitching his head slightly and looked as if he wanted to be anywhere but where he was.

The other two were different. The tall man wearing the striped apron was the town butcher. His hands looked strong enough to tear a steer apart by themselves and his forearms were spotted with dark specks that could have been blood. Alongside him was a shortish man with thinning hair and the black linen suit of a preacher.

Hart wondered if he was the one who'd cut out the tongue of the youngster working the ferry.

'I'm Hansley. Mayor of Guthrie.'

He used his voice like he was talking to a meeting.

Hart leaned back in his chair and nodded, glancing from one

face to another and showing that he didn't give a damn for any of them.

'We represent the citizens of this town and we have regard to the, em, safety of its citizens. As such . . .'

Hart spread both hands out in front of him, cutting the man short. 'You got anythin' to say or you just practisin' for election time?'

The butcher tried and failed to supress a laugh; the preacher looked angry; the pair in suits didn't seem to believe what they'd heard. Hansley reddened and took a half pace backwards, pushing the fingers of his left hand between the buttons of his vest.

'Sir, I . . .'

'You're either goin' to offer me the job of sheriff or advise me to move on through town come morning.'

'I . . .'

'We ain't got no call for a sheriff.' The butcher looked sideways at Hart, pulling at a piece of animal fat that had got stuck to the hairs of his arm.

Hart nodded. 'You provide the meat for the McMurty place?'

The butcher flicked the piece of fat down on to the sawdust. 'Sure do. Why?'

Hart gave a quick grin. 'Good beef.'

The butcher's smile broadened. 'Thanks.'

'We did not come here to discuss meat,' said the mayor, his temper rising.

'Well. Better spit it out then.'

'The ways of the hired gun are the ways of the devil,' said the preacher, clenching his hands fast together. 'And we of this town are determined to make it the most God-fearing in the territory.'

Hart stood up fast, pushing his chair so that it toppled sideways to the floor. Everyone except the butcher jumped back. Hart noticed the bartender move towards what he guessed was a hidden gun under the counter. Quickly he let him see the move had been noticed. The bartender stopped shifting and kept his hands well in sight.

Hart stared at the preacher.

'That your boy out there workin' the ferry?'

'I don't see . . .'

'Is it?'

'Yes, but . . .'

'That how you make folk God-fearing? That the way of God, reverend? Cuttin' out the tongue of your own kin, your own son? If that's what the word of God tells you he ain't talkin' no language I can understand.'

The preacher's face was a mixture of anger and shame; he moved one hand to his face and began to dig the nails of his fingers into the skin of his cheek, making clear, white lines. His breathing was high and whining.

Hart's hand hovered above his gun butt.

The butcher touched the preacher's arm. 'Best leave. Go. We'll handle it.'

He lifted the man's hand from his face and forcibly turned him around; the preacher began to walk towards the doors; Hart let his hand shift to his belt and hooked his thumb inside it, waiting.

'I didn't want to be in on this,' the butcher said, 'but bein' on the town council I didn't have a lot of choice. We voted an', as usual, I lost. Hansley here owns most of the town 'cept my store. Anyhow, these . . .' he paused and looked at them '. . . gentlemen, want to know what you're doin' in Guthrie and aim to persuade you to change your mind if you're thinkin' of settlin'.'

'There's enough lawlessness in the territory without hired guns goin' round advertisin' themselves . . .' began the mayor.

'I ain't exactly been advertisin'.'

'And if we're ever going to get statehood we've got to root out the lawless elements and . . .'

Hart pushed his hand into Hansley's chest and cut him short. 'You're makin' speeches again. I get your drift. I'll be stayin' here a couple of days at most an' unless someone gives me cause, this gun of mine's stayin' in its holster. Just keep that damned fool preacher out of my way.'

The butcher turned towards the doors. 'C'mon, Hansley, let's go. We've got what we came for.'

'Not exactly . . .'

'As close as we're goin' to get. Come on!'

'Listen to what he says,' advised Hart. 'He's the only one of you with his share of common sense, seems to me.'

The mayor bristled and hemmed and hawed but he moved towards the street; as soon as he did the other pair scuttled after him like frightened geese.

Hart waited until the bat wing doors were swinging closed and stepped over to the bar.

'What you got stashed under there?'

'Sawed-off.'

'Thought so. Who were you aimin' usin' it on?'

The barman paused then shrugged: 'Hansley, this place is his. He pays my wages.'

'Pays for killin'?'

'I never said that.'

Hart dropped a couple of coins on to the bar. 'I'm payin' for a bottle of whisky as won't wake me up feelin' like I drank mule's piss.'

The bartender reached behind him. 'Here.'

Hart nodded and walked out. Mrs McMurty hadn't said anything about taking a bottle upstairs to bed.

Four

In fact, Hart felt pretty good. The whisky had been okay, the bed wide and high and even and his dreams hadn't bothered him a damn. He'd woken early and taken a walk down to the livery stable almost before the sun had pushed over the edge of the horizon. Clay looked to be almost as well fed as himself.

Now he was waiting on a plate of breakfast in Eileen

McMurty's dining-room and having trouble in keeping his patience under control. When the food arrived, he grinned at Mrs McMurty like a kid.

'You all right?'

Hart gazed at the mess of eggs, the pork steak and bacon, mushrooms and a pile of buttered wheatcakes.

'Sure,' he said, still smiling. 'Sure, I'm fine.'

'You drinking last night?'

'Some.'

'Huh!' The landlady turned away, happier now she'd discovered a reason for his strange behaviour. There had to be something wrong for a grown man to be grinning like an idiot over his breakfast.

'You want coffee?' The turkey neck wobbled as she swung her head back towards him.

Hart shook his head. 'No, ma'am.'

'No?' The steel-rimmed spectacles twitched a little.

'No coffee, thanks.'

Eileen McMurty went off to the kitchen, shaking her head from side to side and leaving Hart to his meal. He was wiping a piece of wheatcake round the edge of the plate and mopping up egg yolk and pork juice when the door opened and the mulatto came in.

There were no other customers.

The men stared at one another for a few moments before the mulatto came stiffly over and stood by Hart's table.

'You know a man name of Fredericks?'

Hart looked full into the mulatto's face, at the dark skin and the broad nose, the dark eyes that were never quite still. 'No.'

'He's a big man. North-west of here.'

'So?'

Eileen McMurty had come back into the room and was hovering in the background. The mulatto turned towards her and she asked him what he wanted.

'I'm here to talk.'

'This isn't a meeting hall,' she bristled.

'I'll have coffee.'

The woman glanced past him to Hart, who returned her look without expression. She went away to get the coffee; the mulatto sat down.

'Name's Jefferson.'

'Hart. Wes Hart.'

'Feller at the livery stable, he passed the word. Said you might be interested in hirin' on. Said you looked right handy with that Colt there.'

'Depends.'

'This Fredericks, he's a big man. He . . .'

'You keep sayin' that. Get to the point.'

Jefferson started in again but broke off when Mrs McMurty arrived with the coffee.

The mulatto drank some and made a face. 'He owns a lot of land north of the Cimarron, either side of Turkey Creek. You know that way?'

'Chisholm Trail runs through there, don't it?'

Jefferson nodded.

'Ain't that up into the Outlet? Into Cherokee territory?'

Jefferson set down his cup. 'Some. Mostly it's to the south of there. Strays over a little, though.'

'Him bein' such a big man.'

Jefferson looked into Hart's face for some change of expression to go with the sarcasm of his voice, but there wasn't any. Just the same blue eyes showing the same mistrust.

'Fredericks, he's been gettin' trouble. Indians, all kinds. Hell of a lot of rustlers. Law comes by maybe once in every few months an' don't do a damn. He wants some law of his own. Somebody good.'

'Send you out looking, did he?'

The mulatto moved his chair and scratched at the front of his plaid shirt. 'That's right.'

Hart looked at the man's face; he didn't believe him, not exactly. But what he said made a kind of sense. He knew there were men making money from selling grazing land to the Texans driving their cattle north to the rail-heads; he knew that as soon as they left their stock to fatten every rustlin' son-of-a-bitch in the territory would be hummin' round like flies to raw meat; he knew about the Indians.

'What d'you think?'

Hart was thinking that all rustlers weren't necessarily sons of bitches; some of them were daughters. He was thinking of Belle Starr; thinking of her so strongly that he could almost smell her, remember the smell of her body as she stood up close to him and leaned against him.

He said: 'Turkey Creek way?'

Jefferson nodded. 'You interested?'

'Might take a ride up an' see.'

'Good.' Jefferson swung his legs out from under the table and stood up. 'How 'bout today?'

'Hold on now. What's the all-fired hurry?'

Jefferson shrugged. 'Sooner you get up there, sooner you get on the pay roll. I'm ridin' this morning. We could go up together.'

Hart wasn't sure. It was the first thing that had come along and it wasn't nothing like definite. What if he rode up to see Fredericks and nothing came of it? Well, what of it? Guthrie wasn't the most welcoming place around – except for Eileen McMurty's food.

'Okay, What time you leavin'?'

'Soon as you're ready.'

Hart nodded. 'Got to pick up a few things in town. I'll be at the livery stable in an hour.'

'Right.'

The mulatto turned and went out. Hart picked at the inside of his mouth with one finger, pushing a piece of meat down from between his teeth. He was wondering if Mrs McMurty had any apple pie ready in the oven: amongst other things.

The water was grey-blue and the current moved swiftly, bunching choppy waves against the bank. The sun flickered on the white tops of the waves like sudden stars. Higher up the river a blue-winged bird with a yellow beak flew up from a batch of cottonwoods with a raucous screech.

The ferryman had spotted Hart and Jefferson from his hut on the opposite bank and started the ferry over to meet them. Water splashed over on to the flat boards and lay in puddles, glistening.

The preacher's son hauled at the rope, a broad smile crossing his face every time he flexed his muscles. Hart and the mulatto stood alongside their mounts, waiting. As the ferry neared the bank, the ferryman jumped off and half-ran with the tie-rope, looping it fast about a spliced cottonwood trunk. The end of the ferry drove up on to the bank and skewed round.

'Leavin' sooner'n you figured.'

The ferryman stared at Hart, his left shoulder more hunched than ever. 'Didn't take much t' Guthrie, huh?'

Hart nodded and led his horse on to the wet planking, Jefferson following. Jonah watched them closely, the sun reflecting from the sweat that glistened on his arms and across the tops of his shoulders. Hart thought about the youngster's father back in the saloon; thought about that time before, on the kitchen table; the knife . . .

The fair-haired kid he'd seen back at the livery stable – maybe it had happened at around that age. How in hell's name could a man . . . ?

Hart pulled at Clay's rein: how in God's name?

'We got us maybe a day's ride if we keep movin'.'

He realized that Jefferson had said something and that he'd half heard it.

'I say we . . .'

'Yeah, sure.'

Hart nodded and watched as the ferryman unwound the rope. 'Don't seem we're goin' to get no more custom.' He put back his head and chuckled, the unruly sides of his beard and whiskers shaking. He coiled the rope deftly, walking back on board.

'Let's get across, boy.'

The preacher's son secured his hands about the thick rope and braced his legs against the deck for the first pull. Going back they'd be fighting the current part way and it was going to take all of his strength.

The ferry rocked and dipped and for a moment Hart thought it wasn't going to move, but then the end slid further into water and Jonah was hauling hard, hand crossing over hand.

For a time Hart watched him. He put him at around seventeen, maybe a year or so either way. Under his short brown hair his face was round and wide and strangely untroubled. The muscles of his arms and legs were well-developed; no pound surplus on his body.

'You two travellin' together?' asked the ferryman, the coiled tie-rope held in his right hand.

'Yeah.' Jefferson answered, turning towards him.

'Goin' far?'

'No.'

The ferryman laughed and hooked the rope over his hunched shoulder so that he could use his right hand to scratch at his neck. 'Talkative couple, ain't you?'

He moved back to by where the boy was working the ferry across. The river was moving swiftly, trying to break the ferry's passage and take it downstream; every few moments the back of it would start to swivel round and Jonah would have to grit his teeth and check the movement with his weight.

Hart stood alongside his horse, holding the reins just below the neck, every now and then reaching over to pat her on her long, smooth nose. Jefferson was a few feet to his right, staring across the river.

They were midway and a sudden jerk to the side sent a wave of water splashing across Hart's boots. Automatically he stepped back and as he did so his body moved slightly round.

It was enough.

In the corner of his right eye he saw the ferryman, closer behind him than he'd thought, hand pulling something out from inside his coat. Immediately he knew it was a gun.

The ferry slewed viciously and Hart lost his footing; the pistol was in the ferryman's hand and Hart dived flat, calling a warning to Jefferson.

A bullet flew through the space where he'd been seconds before and he heard the ferryman laugh and Jefferson curse and then there was another shot and someone let out a scream of pain.

Hart rolled wide of his horse's legs and pushed himself up into a crouch. The ferryman was steadying his gun with both hands, swaying some as the planking shifted beneath his spread legs. He chuckled, squinted along the barrel of the gun and fired.

Hart threw himself to his left, hand arching downwards towards his Colt. As his left shoulder and hip hit the boards his fingers touched the grip and tightened; he rolled fast and pulled the Colt clear of its holster. Straightening, steadying himself with left hand hard against the planking, he thumbed back the hammer and squeezed the smooth metal of the trigger back against the guard.

There was a double explosion and one shot was his.

The ferryman was hurled back through the air as if he'd been punched in the chest by a steel fist. His feet left the deck and he cannoned into the rump of Hart's mare, which shied and stamped her hoofs. The ferryman sank forwards on to his knees and stared at Hart, who worked the hammer for another shot.

Blood trickled from the edges of the ferryman's mouth and ran through his grey whiskers, staining them bright red. He tried to hold onto his pistol but it fell away and bounced into a shallow puddle, spinning through a slow circle. Hunched, humped, the man gazed at Hart, blinked then coughed. His head went back and he opened his mouth wide; the chuckling laugh was drowned in a splutter of blood.

His head lurched forwards and down and hit the boards with a crack.

Hart swung his gun to the side – Jefferson was lying on his side, both hands pressed to his stomach, legs drawn up close. Like he was sleeping.

And the boy . . . ? The boy . . .

Hart turned again but not fast enough. A bunched fist hammered down on to his gun arm and the pain shot from bone to brain and back. His hand opened and the Colt fell away. The same fist moved fast and caught Hart under the ribs. He went backwards and lost his footing, sliding on the wet, rocking surface.

Jonah jumped, knee angled and driving for Hart's groin. Hart moved fast but not fast enough. The knee drove down into the inside of his thigh and his eyes closed tight with the sharpness of the pain.

His leg went numb.

Hands were at his throat and he flung up both arms and tried to knock them away. The grip was loosened but still held fast. Through Hart's mind flashed the image of the boy's hands tight about the ferry rope. He swung his head sideways and sank his teeth into the boy's wrist. Jonah shouted and let go his grip, swinging a punch with his right hand. Hart ducked inside it and the fist smashed into the deck.

Hart moved his head again and rammed it hard into the boy's face. There was a crunch of bone and Jonah staggered back, blood streaming from his nose. Hart dived. Head and hand sank into Jonah's belly and the two of them landed in a heap by the far side of the ferry.

Hart stepped on the boy's arm and jumped back; the deck moved sideways underneath him and he was almost thrown off balance again. He caught sight of his Colt wedged against Jefferson's curved neck and turned towards it. An arm wound about his neck and something – a knee or a fist – hammered into the small of his back.

He was thrown round and away; saw the side of the deck and the chopping waves of the river beyond; one leg gave underneath him and he threw out his arms. A line before his eyes, blurred and indistinct and then the thick rope was tearing at his throat: tearing: burning.

Hart's body slid through underneath the rope and for seconds he was hanging on it, fibres biting into his neck, the skin under his jaw. The rope burnt his face like fire as he grazed past in, down into the water. The side of the deck thumped into his head. Hart let himself go beneath the surface, drifting down with the current.

When he splashed clear and gasped in air, the ferry was ten yards to his left and moving in the direction of the opposite bank. The preacher's son was yanking on the rope as fast as he could, hand over hand over hand.

Hart shook his head again, gulped in more air and started to swim, fighting the current as it tried to drive him with it.

The heavy ferry was finding the going more difficult than he was. From time to time Jonah would glance round but it needed all his energies to reach the shore.

Hart came level with the back of the deck and struck out more strongly, swimming along the far side away from the rope.

He reached up a hand and clung on: the end of the ferry ground against the bank. Jonah jumped clear with the tie-rope and slithered through the first few feet of mud until he had the thing secured. When he turned Hart was out of the water.

The two stood facing one another. The boy's eyes widened in his round, smooth face and his mouth opened; he made a choked, gutteral sound and charged. The strongly muscled body gleamed. On the end of the ferry, Hart braced himself, hands curved open and outstretched.

As Jonah closed fast, Hart grabbed across for his right arm with his own right hand and swivelled low, throwing his hip into the boy's stomach. There was a crunch of bone and the side of Hart's body jarred; the boy was falling, trying to bring Hart down with him.

Hart evaded one flailing arm and aimed a punch at Jonah's head. The blow landed and it was like hitting rock. A boot kicked into Hart's belly and he went back fast; Jonah rolled and sprang after him. Hart found himself thrown against his own horse and turned so that his face struck the leather of the saddle and cannoned away. Again, the arm slid round his neck and tightened. Sweat and heat. Through the flesh and muscle, the hardness of bone. Choking, grinding back against the skin where the rope had burnt it. Tight. Tight. Tight.

Hart's fingers fumbled blindly for the saddle pommel; closed about the haft of the knife.

He swung his elbow hard into his attacker's stomach and

wrenched his neck sideways – the arm tightened further. Hart's mouth gasped vainly for air. His head throbbed. He struck back again and brought the knife against the arm. The blade sliced through flesh, touching bone. As the elbow moved and the grip loosened, Hart twisted inside it.

He saw the big, open eyes, the staring, uncomprehending face and drove the knife with all his strength, going upwards in a short swing, up between the ribs.

Jonah was jolted backwards and Hart pulled the knife clear. The blade, the front of the boy's shirt, were fresh with blood. Jonah stared at it, unable to believe. He tossed his head and came for Hart again, but Hart side-stepped and struck out with the end of the bone handle clenched tight. The boy went sprawling across the deck and landed on his face. Hart pushed the knife down into his belt and picked up his gun from where it had become wedged under Jefferson's body.

He turned the boy over. Where he had been laying, puddles on the deck had reddened.

'Why? Why d'you do it? Who paid you to do it?'

Jonah shook his head then looked at the body of the ferryman.

Hart knelt in front of him, catching hold of the bloodied front of his shirt. 'Who the hell was it? Who?'

The preacher's son opened his mouth and deep in the red, dark space Hart could glimpse the root of tongue moving vainly. The sounds that emerged were nothing more than that; rehearsals of words which would never be heard.

Hart stood up.

He bent down by Jefferson. The shell had gone in close to the heart and the front of his coat and shirt were matted with blood. Jagged edges of skin and material stuck to one another around the exit wound in his back. Likely he'd been dead before hitting the boards. Hart went through his pockets and found a faded letter he didn't bother to read and a handful of dollar bills. He pushed the bills into his own pocket.

The ferryman had a piece of gold inside a tobacco sack in his pocket. Hart weighed it in the palm of his hand, guessing that what he was doing was weighing the value of his own life. He couldn't put it at more than a hundred dollars. That didn't seem too much to him.

He stood on the ferry, throwing the gold up and down and looking from body to body to body. The preacher's son was stretched out on his back and his eyes were closed; the knife wound in his chest was still seeping blood. Hart thought he was still alive but didn't know how long for.

Hell, he'd made his choice!

He untethered Clay and led the dapple grey up on to the bank. The gold piece was deep in his own pocket. Hart reached out and cut the tie-rope, slipping the knife back into the Indian sheath hanging from the saddle.

Somewhere to the north-west was a man who might give him a job; somewhere also was someone who was willing to pay to see him dead, someone who would kill him himself if he got the chance.

Hart climbed into the saddle and swivelled round: the ferry had started slowly to drift downstream, the sun still picking out the crested heads of waves as the current bore it along.

Five

Turkey Creek ran north to south in a wavering line that took it into the Cimarron. Close by it was the stage line from the Kansas border to Fort Reno on the North Fork of the Canadian River. Either side of the creek was tall prairie grass, the reddish soil showing through close to its banks.

If Fredericks was selling grazing rights, thought Hart, then he'd sure picked a good place to do it. Instead of keeping their herds through the hard Texas winter and then driving them north after the spring round-up, the big ranchers could move the longhorns as far as Indian Territory in the fall and let them winter there, where the climate was kinder. They'd fatten up on that lush prairie grass and the early spring would see the herds pushed the short distance north to the railroad.

And Fredericks sat in the middle and waited for the money to come rolling in. All he needed was a wide, peaceful stretch of range and nothing too much in the way of competition.

Hart lifted the water canteen from his saddle pommel and unscrewed the top. The water was warm and tasted stale. The sun was dipping down behind a low roll of hills far to the west. The land was darkening, closing in as it folded towards the creek valley.

He thought about refilling the canteen but decided against it. Better to reach the Fredericks place before he lost the light. Ten miles back he'd pulled in his horse near a sodbuster's place and asked for directions. At the sound of Fredericks' name the family had gone quiet, cold. The thin, balding father had looked again at Hart's holstered Colt and his saddle guns and then glanced at the long-barrelled Sharps leaning close by his own doorway. The girl with shaved hair had hurried to her mother and pressed close against her long skirts. Two boys stopped sawing wood and stared.

'What's passed between you?' Hart had asked.

The man shook his head. 'Nothing.'

'Only?'

'Only he don't like us here. Don't like our kind gettin' in his hair, messin' with his range.'

'Thought you had a right,' said Hart.

The man spat sideways and pressed his boot down over it. 'Maybe Fredericks got his own ideas as to what's right.'

Hart nodded. One of the boys was moving slowly round towards where the Sharps was resting against the sod wall.

'Tell your boy to stay where he is. I don't want to add to your troubles none.' Hart's voice was soft, easy. The father turned and the son stood where he was, simply looking back at him.

The woman spoke for the first time. She was tall, almost as

tall as her husband; her hair was tied into a tight bundle on top of her head; her arms were wiry and veined, hands pressed against the dark material of her skirt.

'If we tell you how to find Fredericks, how do we know he won't send you back here to throw us off our land?'

'Ma'am,' Hart began, 'neither of us . . .'

'Mary,' interrupted the father, 'he's going to find the place with or without our help.' He turned back towards Hart. 'Go north along the creek another ten or so miles. You'll see a hill with a squarish top off to the west. Head for that. Fredericks' place is a couple of miles on.'

Hart nodded: 'Thanks.'

He raised a hand towards the rest of the family and pulled the grey around. The man stepped towards him.

'One thing. When we come out here it was with a Bible in our hands and God in our heads and hearts. We still got the Bible, only it's back inside. That Sharps is nearer our hands now. You can't beat this land with God alone, we found that out. You do come back here, remember that.'

Hart put out his hand and the man reached up and shook it; it was a good, firm grip.

'I'll remember,' he said.

Hart glanced back once and they were standing as he'd left them, like a tableau, watching.

By the time he reached the turn-off from the creek the sun was setting behind the square hill. Dark clouds moved slowly over it, their undersides lit with orange. Purple-orange light spread about either side of the hill and the top seemed settled with molten fire. As the horizon moved further to each side, the line of light dipped and darkened, sinking through a field of yellow.

Hart reined in Clay and freed his blanket from behind the saddle, slipping it over his body, where the evening cold had been biting into his shoulders.

The Fredericks place was set back against a rise of land, a stream that flowed into Turkey Creek passing close in front of it. When Hart saw it first he could only pick out the outline – a square building, two storeys high. As he rode nearer, details became clearer. Steps at the side of the house, leading up to a door on the first floor. The main door, wide and painted white. Glassed windows set in square criss-crossed frames. At one of these, on the ground floor to the left of the door, a light showed. For a moment Hart glimpsed a figure passing in front of it, between lamp and window.

'Hold it!'

Hart pulled in on the reins, freeing his right hand to drift towards his holster. Someone was standing in front of the low line of buildings away to the far side of the house, barns and such Hart guessed. Beyond them again was the corral.

'Who are you, mister?'

'Come to see Fredericks.'

'That ain't no answer.'

'Maybe it's all your goin' to get.'

He could see him now, stetson angled to one side, wool coat, rifle resting across his left arm. The figure crossed the light inside the house again, deflecting Hart's attention.

'I'm askin' again, who are you? What's your business?'

'I told you, I want to see Fredericks.'

'You see me first.'

Hart sighed; his fingers were touching the smooth leather of the gun belt now, almost on the mother-of-pearl grip of the Colt.

'Man named Jefferson . . .'

'The mulatto?'

'That's him. Told me to ride out an' see Fredericks 'bout a job.'

There was a pause and then the man with the rifle took a couple of paces closer. 'Why don't you get down off that horse of yours?'

'Why don't you put up the rifle?'

The white door swung open and a man came out. 'What's the trouble, Peters?'

'No trouble. This feller just rode in. Said he wanted to see you. Said Jefferson told him to come. No sign of Jefferson, though. I was just checking him out, Mr Fredericks.'

Fredericks looked up at Hart, waited a few moments, thinking. 'Come into the house and we'll talk. Peters, see to his horse.'

Hart waited until the man had put up his rifle and then slid from the saddle and followed Fredericks into the building. There was a small hallway with a wool rug laid down on painted boards, doors to either side. Fredericks opened the door to the left and light spilled out.

'Come in.'

The room was perhaps twenty foot square and carpeted. There were dark green curtains, not drawn, hanging by the windows in the front and side wall. The back wall was lined with book shelves from bottom to top, mostly stacked solid with leather-bound volumes. An oil lamp stood on a central table, swelling smoked glass on a polished brass base. There was another, longer and lower table and three armchairs. The woman in one of the chairs had black hair taken away from her white face into a bun. There was a jewelled slide in the side of her hair and her lips were painted deep red. She was wearing a black dress with a black lace shawl over her otherwise bare shoulders. One leg was crossed over the other beneath the flared skirt of the dress.

She leaned back in the chair and stared openly at Hart, taking in his lean tallness, the Indian blanket that hung diagonally from his right shoulder, the flat-crowned hat angled low, the dust of the trail on his pants and boots and face. The faded blue eyes that were answering her stare.

'This is my wife,' said Fredericks, moving towards her.

'Ma'am,' said Hart nodding with a quick dip of the head.

She opened the fingers of her hand and spread them along the arm of the chair. 'Bonney,' she said. 'Bonney Fredericks.'

Fredericks put his hand on the back of her chair so that it was just touching the lace of her shawl. With a slight shrug she moved her body forward.

'Wes Hart, ma'am.'

He looked past her at her husband. Fredericks was thick-set, a couple of inches under six foot. His dark hair was brushed away from a parting on the right of his head. He had a nose that was a little too large for his face, a mouth that was too small. His cheeks were florid and beginning to sag some with loose flesh.

He was wearing a dark suit flecked with light grey, the buttons of the vest undone. He didn't seem to be carrying a gun.

Hart put him at around forty years of age.

'You said something about Jefferson?' Fredericks asked.

Hart nodded. 'Met him in Guthrie. According to him, you were looking to hire a man. Jefferson seemed to think I might be him.'

Fredericks blinked: 'What kind of man?'

Hart looked at him coolly. 'One that can use a gun.'

Mrs Fredericks moved her hand again, touching it to her other arm.

'Why should I . . . ?'

'He said you were gettin' trouble. Needed someone to sort it out.'

Fredericks stepped away from his wife's chair, turned and looked at her. 'Bonney, would you like to step outside while we discuss this matter?'

The eyes flashed: 'No, Jackson, I don't think I should care to step outside.'

Her body remained relaxed but the words were as taut and dangerous as a length of oiled rope.

Fredericks looked as if he was going to say something in reply, but he thought better of it. Instead he turned back to Hart.

'Where is Jefferson?'

'Dead.'

'You killed him?' It was only just a question.

Hart saw Fredericks slip his right hand into his coat pocket and figured he had a derringer stashed away there.

Hart smiled, the tightest ghost of a smile and let Fredericks see that his hand was now covering the butt of his Colt. 'No, I didn't kill him. Comin' out of Guthrie, someone tried to kill me. Jefferson happened to be around an' got in the way.'

'Convenient.' Fredericks' small mouth curled with sarcasm.

'Not for Jefferson.'

No one said anything for a while. Mrs Fredericks continued to run the tips of her fingers along the shiny skin of her arm;

Fredericks kept his hand on the derringer in his coat pocket, his eyes on Hart. A boot squeaked a loose board close outside.

'You made enemies in Guthrie?' Fredericks said eventually.

Hart shook his head: 'No.'

'Then why . . .?'

'I don't know.'

Bonney Fredericks ceased moving her fingers and pressed them into the soft flesh of her arm. 'It makes you sound like a dangerous man to be around, Mr Hart.'

'That depends, ma'am.'

'What on?'

'What you're intendin' on doin'.'

The woman's eyes widened, dark in the whiteness of her face, stones in snow.

Fredericks turned and went to the low table and poured himself a drink from a glass decanter. He didn't offer anyone else one. He said: 'How do I know you're not some no-good down on your luck and out to take me for whatever you can as soon as my back's turned? How do I know you're as good as you claim to be?' He swallowed half of his drink.' I don't imagine you carry references.' The thin mouth curled once more.

Hart's right hand blurred as his body dropped into a crouch: the Colt .45 was in his hand and the triple click of the hammer being levered back was the loudest sound Fredericks had ever heard. The end of the barrel was pointing directly at the centre of his chest.

There was a slow, low moan of sound as Bonney Fredericks released her breath.

'That's the only reference I've got,' said Hart easily. 'You find someone who's faster, hire him.'

Fredericks and his wife continued to stare at the gun. Something had clotted at the back of Fredericks' throat; his fingers had frozen on the metal of the derringer. Hart released the hammer, returned the gun to its holster.

'I worked with the Rangers down in Texas. Before that rode as an Indian scout. Just handed Fagan back his deputy badge in Fort Smith.'

'Jim Fagan?'

'That's the one.'

'How come you handed in your badge?'

The image of the kid's twisted face at the rope's end rose up in Hart's mind and he touched the burn marks on his own neck with his left hand. It was only the quickest of movements, but Bonney Fredericks followed it closely.

'Let's say we didn't see eye to eye.'

'Mmm.' Fredericks downed his drink. 'So now you want to work on your own?'

Hart nodded. 'You want a regulator, I'm your man.'

Fredericks glanced at his wife; he moved to the shelves and pulled a volume half-way out, glanced at the title and pushed it back.

'We'll give it a trial. One month. Pay'll be sixty . . .'

'Hundred.'

'That's . . .'

'Hundred a month. Take it or leave it. I'm the one who's likely to get himself killed. All you have to do is pay to set me up.'

Bonney Fredericks smiled; she uncrossed her legs and smoothed down her dress.

'Okay,' said Fredericks. 'A hundred. But on a one month trial, mind.'

Hart nodded.

'Would that be with all found?' asked the woman, the smile now held in her dark eyes.

Hart looked down at her and the smile moved up and down his body. 'Yes, ma'am, I guess it would.'

Fredericks rammed the heel of his hand into the side of her chair, jolting it round. 'Bonney, I asked you before and now I'm telling you. You leave business affairs to me! I'll handle them my own way.'

She moved her hands away from the sides of the chair, adjusted the lace shawl, stood up. In the glow of the oil lamp, the pallor of her face took on a sudden sheen.

'Well, Jackson,' she said softly, arching the upper part of her body towards him. 'I guess you have to prove to yourself you can still handle something.'

Fredericks flinched as if he'd been struck and then he swung his right hand, fingers extended, right into the side of her face. Into and across it, knocking her head back so that Hart could only see the tightly drawn hair and the jewelled slide.

Fredericks moved as if he might hit her again, breath coming noisily through his nostrils, cheeks redder and more flushed than before. After a few moments he let his hand fall by his side; he was chewing away at the inside of his mouth, the right cheek moving in and out.

The imprint of his fingers stood out clearly on Bonney Fredericks' pale face; deep red lipstick had been smeared away from one corner of her mouth. Her hands were clenched tight together; her eyes burned darker, deeper than before.

Hart had not moved. His glance went from one to the other of them, wondering if this were a usual eruption of anger or if it had been building up slowly for some time.

Mrs Fredericks shifted her gaze to Hart. He was unable to tell what she was thinking, feeling. She said: 'Good night, Mr Hart. Doubtless I shall see you again.'

She said it calmly, evenly, as if nothing had happened. Without saying a word to her husband, she turned with a swirl of her dress and left the room.

Fredericks went back to the decanter and poured a drink, larger than the first. This time he poured one for Hart as well.

'Sit down.'

Hart sat in the chair Mrs Fredericks had left, hanging his hat from one corner. When he laid his arm along one side he could feel the warmth her body had left behind.

'My wife . . . she doesn't always think what she's saying. It's being out here on the prairie. No one much to talk to.' He shifted the glass between both hands. 'She's a . . . she's a good woman.'

He looked at Hart earnestly. Hart didn't say anything but he didn't believe it, either. Whatever Bonney Fredericks might be –

and she was likely a lot of things – a good woman wasn't one of them.

Fredericks drank some, fiddled with the glass a little more, got up and fetched a cigar box from between the rows of books. He held it out to Hart who declined with a shake of the head.

'You ever been married?'

The question caught Hart like a rattler under a stone. He didn't know how long it was before he answered, 'No,' but it seemed a long time.

Fredericks nodded and exhaled a ring of smoke which drifted towards the ceiling, changing shape and breaking into formless patterns as it went.

'Jefferson told you the situation?'

'Way I see it, you got a parcel of land doin' nothin' but growin' good grass and you're sellin' grazin' rights to any Texas trail boss who wants his stock to fatten up through the winter. Come spring you get 'em to the railroad and lop off a share of the profit.'

'You say it as though you don't like it.'

'I don't have to like it.'

Fredericks drew on the cigar. 'That's right. You don't. All you have to do is keep any trouble right away from my land.'

'You make it sound easy.'

'It's not easy. Unless you're as good as you say you are.'

Hart leaned forward. 'We'll see 'bout that. Where do I start?'

'First herd's due in a couple of weeks, depending on the weather. Soon as they arrive there'll be rustlers comin' out of the hills like worms out of the woodwork. I want them shown the error of their ways.'

Hart's fingers clenched and unclenched. 'No lynchin'.'

'Why in the Lord's name not?'

'I ain't partial to it.'

'Partial! What the deuce has that got to do with anything?'

'I'll do things my way. There's more than hangin' to warn men off.'

Fredericks stood up and set the empty glass on the table by the lamp. 'Every steer that gets rustled, that costs me money. You remember that.'

'I'll remember it.'

Hart stood up and faced Fredericks, staring at him until the other man looked away. The smell of cigar smoke was strengthening in the room.

'Taylor and the other men sleep in the bunkhouse outside. There's a spare bunk there.'

Hart grinned and shook his head.

'What . . .?'

'You got a spare room upstairs, ain't you? Place this size.'

Fredericks squeezed the cigar, almost breaking it into pieces. 'Damn it, man! You'll sleep out with the rest of the hired men.'

Hart hooked his thumbs into his gun belt. 'I won't. I won't 'cause if I do they'll think I'm the same as them an' that might not be best. An' I won't 'cause I ain't just another hired hand, I'm your regulator. An' at a hundred dollars a month I deserve a good bed.'

He turned towards the door, hesitated, swung back. 'A few more things while we're gettin' straight. You see that Peters and whoever else you got out there know that if I need 'em to do somethin' they do it. An' however you think you can get away with treatin' that wife of yours, don't waste your time tryin' the same on me – an' that includes any ideas you might have concernin' that fancy gun you've got stashed in your coat pocket.'

He stepped past Fredericks and scooped up the decanter. 'It'd help if you stopped bein' so damned mean with your brandy.'

Hart shut the door hard with his right hand and stepped outside the house. Peters was standing close by, rifle resting against his body. He tensed when Hart came out and slipped his hand down to the trigger guard.

'My bags and saddle guns,' Hart said. 'Get 'em. I'll be upstairs.'

Peters stared back at him through the dusk, as if not quite able to take in what had been said. But as Hart didn't move or speak again, he slowly moved away towards the barn.

Hart leaned against the doorway, decanter trailing from the fingers of his left hand, right hand at his belt close by the butt of the Colt. Every vestige of light had disappeared from the sky.

Six

The eyes were hazel tinged with green, the hair brown, long, falling around her face, across her face. Tears bitten back, welling again inside. He reached out to touch her and she pulled away, turning her head from him as if his hand upon her would be like touching something rotted and old.

'Kathy!'

The face muscles tightened, the tears set away, there was nothing there but pain and strength.

'Kathy!'

Hart heard the word and woke, startled by the sound of his own voice. Through the open window he could see a pattern of stars, forking left to right across the blackness. Strand of her hair left to right across her face – freckled face. Cold sweat lay on him like a skin. He sat up in the bed and wiped at his arms with the flannel sheet, at his arms, chest, face and neck, the insides of his thighs.

He knew what had brought the dream back to his mind. Fredericks' question: have you ever been married? No, he could have said. No. I just stood in the place I built for her, for the pair of us to live in and watched her telling me that she wasn't going to live there, that she wasn't going to marry me. That was all. As close as he'd come to being married. A handful of years ago, not much in a life. Long enough for a dream to become a nightmare.

Before Kathy there had been women enough, more than enough. Saloon girls and whores and chance encounters whose names he couldn't remember even if he'd ever known them. Since then the only person who might have meant anything to him had been Carol Peterson, a woman he'd spoken to for half an hour.

Hart thought about the strangely neat, ordered cabin deserted by people and wondered again where she and her husband might have gone, what might have happened to them. He recalled the look on her face when she'd talked of having children – later – one day. Remembered smoothing rough-hewn wood to satin in the room that would have been for his and Kathy's firstborn.

A son.

Why a son?

Was it only so that when he was gone there would still be someone else that was still part of him? Blood of his blood. Was that it? Flesh of his flesh. Like the boy he'd had to kill on the ferry, the one whose father had cut out his tongue. Like his own father, coming home from his prospecting trips with nothing to show for it but an aching body and a bloody temper.

Is that what it meant – father and son?

If so, wasn't he better off as he was?

Hart lay back down and pulled the covers over his shoulders. He closed his eyes and tried to empty his mind and drift back to sleep.

Hart spent the first few days getting to know the extent of the Fredericks property and lay of the land. He also talked with the men Fredericks kept on his regular payroll – he would take on extra hands when there were herds to drive up to the border.

Peters didn't prove any less surly and difficult to get on with after Hart got to know him a little. A stocky wrangler with a drooping brown moustache and a greasy stetson that he never seemed to take off, Peters was only half-way civil to Hart because he knew his job depended on it. But every chance he got he made it clear as day that he reckoned Hart was only slightly preferable to a wild dog.

He was five or six years the older man and he'd spent his life since fourteen handling broncs and steers and bustling his way to be top hand. When the trail herds came through he'd be worth double his pay but until that time, he just riled Hart all the time, as if driving him to swing a punch. Hart let it ride and kept out of Peters' way as much as he could. The time might come when he'd need to have him on his side.

Chavez was a Mexican who'd drifted up from Texas a year before and stuck around. He was tall for a Mex, a few inches above six foot and rangey with it. He wore one of those leather vests studded with pieces of polished metal that Mexicans seemed to like and a large-brimmed sombrero. He spoke in a broken accent that Hart suspected he put on more than he needed to and liberally sprinkled what he said with odd words of Mexican.

Whenever he was sitting around doing nothing much, he'd take out his knife – a slim-bladed throwing knife with a double edge like a razor – and toss it over and over, always catching it with the haft in the palm of his hand. Every now and then he'd punctuate this routine by throwing it at anything that moved close. One time Hart saw him impale a long-legged spider from a dozen feet, the contents of the insect's sac spilling out around the blade.

The other two were called T.C. and Howie. They'd been signed on together when they came up the Chisholm Trail that spring. Howie had had a run-in with the trail boss and got himself fired. T.C. had quit on the spot and drawn his pay. They'd worked for Fredericks ever since. Howie was a barrel-chested man with legs that seemed too small for the rest of his body. He had a wide-open face and the look of someone who was constantly being taken by surprise. T.C. was taller and thinner and had a habit of coughing into an old red kerchief he always carried with him – long, racking coughs which bent him near double and took the blood from his face. He had only three fingers on his left hand; the middle two had got smashed up when he was tossed from a bronc that followed up by stomping him against a corral fence. The fingers had been so torn and crushed the foreman had given T.C. a quick slug of whisky and cut through them close to the knuckle with a big old bowie knife.

Hart had ridden out with Howie and T.C. a few times – north towards the Salt Fork of the Arkansas River, west towards the hills that led into the Outlet. To the east the tree line began and the prairie got swallowed up in oak. Southwards was the Canadian River.

It was at the end of one of these journeys that Hart got back to find Fredericks with visitors. Three Cheyennes were astride their ponies outside the house, two wearing leggings and breech cloths, one a pair of wool pants several sizes too large. All three had hide shirts decorated with quillwork and beads. Their hair was greased and pulled back on their heads, parted at the centre.

Peters was standing outside the bunk house, toying with his rifle. Chavez was sitting on the ground by the end of the barn, throwing his knife up into looping circles.

Hart nodded for T.C. and Howie to ride to the left and went slowly forward. The Cheyenne who turned to face him had a nose that looked to have been broken more than once and spread across his face. He was nursing a Winchester in both hands, letting it rest on his thighs. The other two were also armed, though with pistols. All three weapons looked new and hadn't lost their shine.

Hart reined in Clay next to the two riderless horses, one another Indian pony, the other a saddled gelding with a white mark on its rear right leg.

Hart got down from his mount carefully, watching the Cheyenne all the time. Their faces regarded him impassively. He went to the door and pushed it open, stepped inside.

Bonney Fredericks was so close inside the door that he was next to her almost before realizing she was there. Something in his head jumped and his hand rested on his gun. She said nothing, looking up at him with her deep-set eyes, a strange half smile on the corners of her painted mouth.

'You aren't going to use that, are you?' She was looking now at his hand on the Colt.

Hart ignored her question and made to step past her. She slid her body into his way and for a moment her bare arm touched his chest.

'Where's Fredericks?'

She turned her head sideways. 'In there. Talking with his Indian friends.'

'What about?'

Her eyes widened in mock surprise. 'You don't really expect me to know. You heard my husband telling me business was none of my affair.'

Hart looked at the side of her face, as if for a moment expecting the marks of Fredericks' hand still to be there, imprinted. Then he moved away and knocked on the door, stepping into the room without waiting for an answer.

Fredericks was standing behind a long dining-table, a cigar in one hand. A white man in a fringed leather jacket and black wool pants was standing close beside him. Opposite them was another Cheyenne, wearing a mixture of white and Indian clothes. Two eagle feathers stuck up at a low angle from the right side of his hair.

On the table were a bottle of whisky, three glasses and a map. The map had been unrolled and two of the glasses were holding down corners; the man alongside Fredericks was keeping down a third corner.

'Anything wrong?' asked Fredericks sharply.

Hart shook his head. 'I was goin' to ask you the same.'

The two men stared at one another for a few seconds and then Hart took a couple of paces towards the table, looking at the map. He saw the area he'd been riding for the past days, the creek, the stage stations, the words in copperplate script – *Ceded to the Cherokee Nation.* Lower down – *Lands set aside for the Cheyenne. Unratified agreement of 18 November 1873.*

'Gentlemen,' said Fredericks, 'this is Wes Hart. He's working for me as regulator. Hart, this is John Probert, he's an Indian Agent in the Cheyenne Nation. And that's Bear-Who-Runs, he's a Cheyenne chief.'

Hart nodded at both men, taking them in quickly. Probert was in his fifties, close to six foot and starting to get a stoop and a belly at the same time. Grey hair and a grey, almost white, moustache. A Colt Peacemaker with a wooden butt and a short barrel holstered by his right hip.

The Cheyenne was older, though it was almost impossible to tell how old. His skin was dark, close to black; the veins on his hands stood out like purple-black worms leeched to his skin. He looked at Hart with brown, still eyes, studied him for a few moments and then turned his head away.

'We were discussing grazing rights,' said Fredericks. 'It seems the Cheyenne feel they have some claims that aren't being met.'

Probert raised a hand above the map and glanced at Hart.

'Pretty straightforward. This parcel of land here . . .' A finger prodded the map. '. . . originally belonged to the Cheyenne by government treaty. In July of sixty-six it was ceded back by the Cheyenne Nation and nothing much has been done with it since. It forms part of what are called the unassigned lands, north and east of Fort Reno. Not many whites have settled the land, mainly 'cause it's surrounded by Indians and they don't sleep too safe at nights.'

He gave a short laugh and grinned over at Bear-Who-Runs, who stared back with the same imperturbable expression.

'But the land's good for grazing as Fredericks found out. Him and a few others. Thing is,' he glanced at Fredericks quickly, 'the more land you use the more beef you can take on, an' the more beef you take on the more money you get back.'

Fredericks stubbed out the end of his cigar. 'All you're saying is obvious. It's business, pure and simple.'

It occurred to Hart that however simple it might be, none of the businessmen he'd come into contact with were what he'd call pure. But he let it slide and said nothing.

Probert was poking down at the map again. 'Thing is, the north-west section of what Fredericks is claiming for his land is inside the area still granted to the Cheyenne by treaty.'

'Which the Cheyenne don't use,' Fredericks put in hastily, anger beginning to show in his voice.

'Which the Cheyenne don't use a whole lot, I agree. On account of it bein' a long way from what's now their homeland and only used for the odd huntin' party.'

'Don't anybody else live on the land?' asked Hart.

'Sure. Arapaho mostly.'

'And I've as much right to it as they have,' said Fredericks. 'More.'

'That's as maybe.' Probert looked straight at him. 'But it ain't the issue.'

Hart moved round the table and poured himself a shot from the whisky bottle into one of the glasses. When he picked it up, a section of the map sprang into a curve.

'How much you asking?'

'Fifty cents a steer.'

Hart pursed his lips, nodded slowly, looked at Fredericks.

'I told you, it's out of the question.'

Bear-Who-Runs turned from the table and stepped around Hart, heading for the door. Probert and Fredericks looked at one another, the Indian Agent fingering the buckle of his belt.

'Hold on,' called Fredericks and the Cheyenne chief turned round slowly.

'I'll make it twenty five.'

After a slight pause the chief shook his head, looking at Probert as he did so.

'Fifty,' repeated Probert.

Fredericks paced away from the table to the far wall and back again, lips moving silently as he did calculations inside his head. Finally he leaned against the table end and planted his fingers down on to it, hands spread wide.

'Forty a head and twenty-five for steers under two.'

Probert straightened up, glancing at the Cheyenne for his approval. Bear-Who-Runs said nothing; after several seconds he gave the slightest nod of his head.

Probert let out a low, whistling breath. 'You got a deal,' he said to Fredericks.

Fredericks stood across the table from the Indian Agent and shook his hand. He went to the roll-top desk at the far side of the room and took out several sheets of paper, a glass bottle of ink and a quill pen. Hart reckoned he'd had enough. Without a word he stepped round the Cheyenne and left the room.

Outside the house, the Indian with the wedge nose stared at him with a lot of hostility, gripping his new rifle as though he'd dearly like to use it. Hart couldn't quite understand why, unless he knew what was going down inside.

Peters and Chavez were still roughly where they'd been before, still looking as if they were expecting trouble to break out at any moment. Hart went past them, leading his horse towards the barn.

Howie was inside, sitting on an upturned oaken bucket and trying to fix a broken bridle.

'What's goin' on?'

Hart shook his head. 'Nothin'. 'Cept business.'

When the Cheyenne made to leave some half an hour later, Fredericks and Probert shook hands again outside the door of the house. All smiles. They hadn't passed out of hailing distance when Hart was inside, facing up to Fredericks across a rolled-up map and a copy of a handwritten contract.

'What gave you the right to barge in here like that?'

'You'd rather do your dirty work without too many folk lookin' on.'

Fredericks started chewing the inside of his mouth. 'Damn it! You were here. You saw what happened. You saw how they pushed me. Way, way over the price I had in mind.'

'Bullshit!'

Hart reached for the nearly-empty bottle and poured himself a shot of whisky. He slid the bottle in Fredericks' direction, but it was ignored.

'Hart, you're not being paid to interfere with my business, you're . . .'

'I know, I'm bein' paid to aim this Colt of mine in whatever direction you want me to point it. But when those Cheyenne wake up to the fact that you're screwin' 'em for one hell of a lot, maybe I just ain't goin' to be enough to stop 'em wipin' you out.'

Fredericks' cheeks were no longer tinged with red, they were glowing with it. The fingers of his hands were clenched so tight his nails had to be cutting into the skin.

'That was a perfectly honest deal. I . . .'

Hart put down the glass with a smack on the hardwood table. There were a whole lot of things about to leap off Hart's tongue but he choked it back.

Fredericks' small mouth was slightly open, his nostrils dilated. The colour was draining from his face now, veins showing through his loose skin.

'I've met a whole lot of Indian Agents an' I only ever met one good one an' he was a Quaker. The rest of 'em are in it for what they can get and they don't give a couple of damns about the

Indians they're supposed to be lookin' out for. Probert don't seem no better.

'All that stuff in here was set-up. Lettin' on that he was forcin' you into a bargain when you'd already agreed it beforehand. They could have got another ten, maybe fifteen cents a head for grown cattle. Do in other parts. So you slipped Probert a hundred dollars and he agreed to go through that act. Bear-Who-Runs might have been fooled an' he might not, but I wouldn't bet on it if I was you. Indians ain't stupid, you know.'

Fredericks backed off towards the desk and then turned. 'That's where you're wrong. They don't think right, they're like children. Savage children. That's why I had to do a deal with Probert. Sign a paper with an Indian and inside a month he's going back on everything he said. You should know that, you were an Indian scout.'

'Only Indians I knew ever went back on their word had damn good reason. They got a brand of honour stronger'n that of most white folk I ever met.'

Fredericks pushed his hands down on to the table and stared hard at Hart. 'What the hell's that supposed to mean?'

'It means I ain't met too many men like you, but I seen enough to know what's chewin' on your gut. You want to own more than anyone else around; you want to own it and control it. I can read it in what you do an' what you say.' Hart stepped over towards the side of the room. 'One thing no Indian's got eatin' away at him an' that's greed.'

Fredericks ground out the end of his cigar and reached for the whisky bottle, pouring himself a strong shot and downing half of it in one. Hart could see him trying to control his reactions and fight down his anger.

Finally he looked at Hart and spoke. 'That's a fancy speech for a gunman, Hart. Fancy words for a hired killer selling his services to the highest bidder.'

Fredericks thumped the table; his voice rose a couple of octaves, the redness of his cheeks deepening.

'Who in God's name do you think you are? You won't see a man with a rope round his neck good and legal, but you'll shoot him down yourself. You try to tell me how to run my business like you was some kind of saint.'

The fist struck the table again, jolting one of the glasses over so that it spun round then rolled through a series of arcs.

'That's a gun you tote in that holster, you know. It ain't no bible. You'd best remember that. Nothing about you give you any right to push your morals on someone else. Especially not me.'

Hart's mouth was set in a tight line, his eyes narrowed; a vein at the left side of his head was beginning to beat. Fredericks stared at him and all of the words that came to him were useless in reply. Maybe what Fredericks said was right; maybe there wasn't much to choose between them; maybe in their own ways they were equally as rotten. But . . .

Fredericks thumbed open a box and picked out a fresh cigar. He struck a match on the table edge and cut off the cigar end with a small knife he kept in his vest pocket.

'Seems to me like we finished our business for now, Hart. You can go.'

Bonney Fredericks was outside the door when Hart stepped through. She made no pretence to hide the fact that she'd been an interested listener. Her eyes swept over Hart's body with a sense of power borrowed from her husband. Hart went quickly past her and out of the house.

Seven

The rider sent up clouds of dust into the bright blue of the sky. The sun sparkled off his spurs, the movement of his bridle. When he slewed his mount round in the space between the Fredericks place and the barn, a whole shower of fresh dust rose to cover him.

The horse reared up on its hind legs and the cowboy dropped from the saddle before it had righted itself again. He whipped off his steep-crowned Texas hat and wafted it through the air.

Fredericks came towards him from the house, Peters and Howie from the barn. Hart leaned against the corral fence and waited.

'Hot damn! It's sure good to see you!'

The cowboy pumped Fredericks' hand and clapped a dusty hand to his sleeve.

'Hot damn an' the devil!'

He was wearing wide batwing chaps, fastened tight behind his dark woollen pants; the rowels on his work spurs spun a little and jingled as he moved; the raised heel of his fancy boot ground the dirt.

'How far you ahead of the herd?'

'Three, maybe four hours.'

Fredericks' face broke into a smile and he looked over to his right. 'Peters! Ride down there with the others. Show them the pasture over east of here.'

He turned back to the cowboy. 'It's not the same place as last fall, but there's better grass. Even better.' His smile broadened. 'First come, first served.'

'That's damn right!'

The cowboy gave Fredericks another slap on the arm and swung round to greet Peters with a firm hand shake. Then he pulled himself up into his saddle and moved the horse forwards then sideways, laughing at his fancy stepping.

Wes Hart came slowly over towards the house.

'Merv,' said Fredericks stepping forward. 'This here's Wes Hart. He's my regulator. Merv Griffiths. His father owns the C Circle down below Austin.'

Griffiths stopped showing off with his horse and looked down at Hart through the swirling dust. Hart waited until the air had cleared, then nodded curtly. Griffiths just stared. His face was young behind a light brown moustache and a scar over his left cheekbone. His eyes were blue, not the faded blue of Hart's, but bright, nervy.

'Since when have you needed one of his kind?' Griffiths asked, leaning sideways in the saddle, half looking at Fredericks while not taking his eyes fully off Hart. All the high humour had left him.

Fredericks made a calming gesture with his hands. 'No need to trouble you boys any. But we get rustlers coming round as soon as the herds start moving in for the winter. With Hart here, you're less likely to lose stock.'

'Thought you had some reg'lar law up here now?'

'There's a US marshal, but he's riding a few hundred miles of territory. No way he can handle things himself, not even with deputies. We have to make our own arrangements.'

Merv Griffiths patted his horse's flank and straightened up, resettling his stetson. 'Just so long as it stays that way an' he don't come to interferin' with us none. My pa sure wouldn't take to that.'

Hart came forward fast, right alongside Griffiths. He set his left hand on the leather of his stirrup, keeping the right free. Griffiths had a pistol holstered behind the edge of his chaps.

'We'll just see what your pa'll take later on. You tell him I'll be out to see him soon as he's settled in. Just a friendly word.'

Griffiths swung his leg and knocked Hart's hand away. Hart stepped back and his body began to dip into a crouch; his hand curved above the butt of his Colt; his eyes met those of the cowboy and held.

'You best get home to your daddy, boy, and tell him what Mr Fredericks an' I said. Fore you forget it.'

Griffiths started to move his right arm back, the hand leaving the reins and shifting away from the saddle pommel. But he hadn't stopped staring into Hart's eyes and what he saw there stopped him.

With a holler he rocked his body in the saddle and dug in his spurs; the horse reared quickly and then started off away from the house.

Hart turned and watched him go, relaxed again, thumbs back inside his belt.

'You didn't need to needle him that way.'

Hart turned and as he did realized for the first time that Bonney Fredericks was standing behind her husband, in the doorway.

'Maybe not.'

But he wasn't looking at Fredericks. She was wearing a black split riding skirt and a white blouse that was tight at the neck and close to her body. Her hair was pulled back just the way it had been before, only this time there wasn't any make-up on her mouth.

She looked back at Hart, his face and the length of his body.

Fredericks was saying: 'No need in getting them all riled up.'

Hart nodded. 'I'll take a ride out there later, like I said. When they've got the herd settled down.'

Fredericks started to argue, but reconsidered. He went over to talk with Peters instead. Hart and Bonney Fredericks looked at one another through the space he had filled just before; then she strode away to the barn to fetch her horse. Hart turned his head slowly and watched her.

From the hill it was possible to see nearly the whole herd, around eight hundred head Hart figured, stretched out in a wide, wavering line. They'd been travelling for a long time and man and beast were tired through. Only the thought of being so near to the end of the journey gave some of them, like Merv Griffiths, a fresh burst of energy. And tired all the same, as soon as the steers smelt the water of Turkey Creek clearly they'd be hard to hold. Wanting them on the other side of the water anyway, Hart guessed the cowhands would let them run.

Hart pushed back his stetson so that it fell behind his head, fastened on the thin cord about his neck. The marks from the ferry rope were still there, the memory of them even clearer. He thought about the two attempts on his life and whether whoever had been responsible had given up or if he would try again. When? How?

Hart rubbed his hand across his stubbled cheek and shook the thoughts clear. Below him he could see the pattern of the drive as the front animals veered off to the west.

Two men rode point, one on either side, the steers a dozen or so abreast at the front. Behind them came the swing and flank riders, constantly moving, turning, using their ropes to keep any cattle from straying too far out of the bunch. The chuck wagon was over to the side, the remuda being driven along behind it by a couple of wranglers.

Hart knew the men riding drag were somewhere at the back of the herd but it was impossible to pick them out through the accumulation of dust that rose up over the rear of the drive like a thick cloud that even the sun couldn't pierce.

Two men rode between swing and point on the left and he guessed they were Griffiths and his father, though there was no way of being certain. The mount that one of them was riding, a soft black, looked like the one Merv Griffiths had been showing his paces on earlier. He wondered what words the boy had passed on about himself and what kind of reception he'd get when he went down later.

Something pulled his head round to the line of hills to the east, where a sparse run of trees caught the redness of the sun. He wasn't the only one watching the herd.

Even at that distance he could tell it was Bonney Fredericks. Her white blouse signalled to him across a half a mile of grass that rose and fell with the contours of the land.

She knew that he had spotted her and turned in her saddle to face him, but gave no further sign. For a moment Hart thought of riding across to where she was but a shout from below shook the idea from his mind. The cattle at the head of the drive had picked up the scent of fresh water strong and clear and they weren't going to be denied.

With curved, lowered horns and stomping hoofs they broke into a charge, the expert riders at the point keeping up with them, swinging their ropes and hollering all the way.

The urgency ran through the herd like a tidal wave. Hart saw the driver of the chuck wagon move it wide; the wranglers rode around the remuda, keeping the riderless horses clear. The man he had guessed to be Griffiths galloped his mount towards the head, waving his hat side to side over his horse's neck, calling orders.

The leading steers raced from sight and the rest were swallowed up in a huge, moving swirl of dust and a thunderous crescendo of sound. Hart watched the C Circle men handling the charging herd and knew what they were doing was difficult as all hell. One false move, one lapse of concentration and a man could be out of his horse's saddle and being tramped to death under hundreds of hoofs.

He'd tried it for a while and pulled back fast.

Thirty a month and found.

He didn't like the pay and he didn't like being just one of a crew. Even when he'd spent his years with the Rangers, the discipline of riding and working in a group had driven him real sore. Alone was how Hart worked best – how he lived best.

He turned his mount round with a pull at the reins: it was how he had to live best.

Little Joe, the wrangler, was called out with the rest;
Though the kid had scarce reached the herd
When the cattle stampeded, like a hailstorm they fled
And left us all a-riding for the lead

Hart rode Clay round the edge of the cattle at a slow walk, listening to the voice of the night herder drift lazily through the air. The moon was three-parts full and bright in the sky, The horns and backs of some of the steers shone eerily, strangely, with an almost glow.

Next morning at day break we found where his horse fell,
Down in a washout twenty feet below;
Beneath his horse, mashed to a pulp, his spur rung the knell
Of the little Texas stray, poor Wrangling Joe

A cowhand wearing a slicker and a tied-down stetson looked suspiciously at Hart from the back of his horse, letting his hand rest on the butt of the carbine in its saddle scabbard. Hart nodded in his direction and carried on past, moving towards the glow of the camp fire.

Another herder was whistling, the first man's song having died away. The tune wavered and cracked and broke; a few moments later it set off again, softer than before. Hart pulled at his Indian blanket which was draped across his body; the night air was cold and would get colder as the hours wore on.

The light from the fire had separated out into three different fires, three different lights. Figures leaning back against their saddles turned and watched, weighing the stranger up.

Hart rode between groups of men and over to the central fire, before the chuck wagon. Two men rose and stood beyond the flames – one was Merv Griffiths, the other his father.

Wes Hart got down from the saddle slow.

'You're Fredericks' regulator – that it?'

'That's right. An' you're Griffiths.'

'Yeah.'

He was an inch or so taller than his son, and heavily built. He still had on worn leather chaps and, despite the cold, only a leather vest over his shirt. A high-peaked stetson was pushed back on his head and what hair was visible was mostly steel grey. A Colt Frontier was tied down low on his right leg.

'Told your boy I'd be comin' out.'

Griffiths looked at him keenly.

'So you're here.'

'Uh-huh.'

Behind him, Hart was aware of men shifting quietly; maybe to get a better view, but maybe to ease a pistol out from underneath their saddle bags.

'How long you an' your men figurin' on stayin' around?'

'No longer'n we need to. I'll come by tomorrow an' get things settled with Fredericks, then we'll be headin' back. How many hands he got now?'

'Four. Takin' on some more in a few days.'

Griffiths nodded.

'You payin' your boys soon as you've dealt with Fredericks?' asked Hart.

'That's what I've said.'

'Not too many places for 'em to spend it out here.'

'Some of 'em 'll ride by one of the stage stations an' get drunk fast. Buffalo or Baker's. Some'll ride on down to Fort Reno. They'll all drift back to Texas in their own time.'

'When they're broke.'

'I don't see what damn business it is of yours.' Merv Griffiths came a pace closer to the fire. The light from the flames reflected in his eyes, showed the scar on his face clearly. His hand was by his hip, not far from his pistol butt.

'Merv, take it steady,' said his father.

'Boy,' said Hart, turning to him, 'I've seen cowhands when they get paid at the end of a long drive. If there's a town around they go roarin' in and whoop it up for a couple of days until they're so drunk and drained they can't but think of ridin' home. But out here in the Territories it ain't like that. There ain't no big saloons, no whorehouses. These men are likely to be chompin' on the bit like broncs that've been roped in the corral too long.'

'I still don't see how that's your business.'

'Anyone steps too far out of line, it's my business.'

'So what you sayin'?'

'Boy, I said it. You keep your ass in line like the rest of your pa's hands or I'll bust you for it.'

'You . . .!'

Merv Griffiths stepped back again and curved his right arm outwards. Hart dropped into a slight crouch, hand covering the butt of his Colt. Griffiths moved faster than he looked able. He was between the two of them, his face set hard and staring at his son, gripping him by both arms.

'What the hell you doin'? You want to get your fool self killed?'

'I'm not goin' to be talked down to like I was some snot-nose kid.'

'Boy, while you're behaving like that, a snot-nose kid is all you are.'

Merv winced as though his father had slapped him in the face;

he pulled himself clear and moved away from the fire fast. Half a dozen paces on he stopped suddenly, turned fast.

Hart was still watching him and his hand was still inches above his Colt.

Merv Griffiths pointed his finger, jabbing the night air. 'You ain't gettin' away with treatin' me like that. You just ain't!'

He turned again and hurried beyond sight. Hart relaxed and straightened. Griffiths sighed.

'You want some coffee?'

'Sure.'

Hart came round the fire and sat cross-legged, slackening the knot on the blanket and warming his hands in front of the flames. The cook handed him a tin cup, full to the brim, and gave another to Griffiths. The hot, black coffee spilled over on to Hart's fingers and near burnt them. When he drank some it did the same to his mouth.

'Got pinto beans an' bacon,' said the cook. 'You want some?'

'They as hot as this?' asked Hart, looking at the man's grizzled face.

The cook chuckled and rubbed his hands together. 'Hotter.'

'I'll pass.'

'I'll take some more,' said Griffiths.

'Okay.' The cook went back to the big cooking pots, blackened and greased with use. The Little Mary, a boy who looked twelve but was likely nearer fourteen, rattled a large spoon and began to pile beans on to a tin plate.

'You ain't got a trail boss?' asked Hart.

'Started off with one. Rattler bit him south of the Red River. Right in the neck. Tried to suck it out, couldn't cut it, not where it was. He was dead in a couple of hours. Since then I've been doin' the job myself. Tryin' to teach Merv, only . . .'

He stopped and took the plate of food from the Little Mary with a nod of thanks.

'Only he don't learn too well. Don't take to being told.'

'What kids do?'

'Yeah.'

Hart drank some more coffee. One of the night herders had started to sing again, high and plaintive.

'You got any kids?'

Hart shook his head slowly. 'No.'

'Uh-huh. Sometimes I think it's prob'ly as well.'

Hart nodded again but said nothing, poking at the edges of the fire with the heel of his boot.

'Hope he's got sense enough to keep out of your way,' said Griffiths after a few moments.

Hart turned his head and looked at him. 'So do I,' he said. 'So do I.'

Eight

At first Hart thought it was still night. When he stepped outside the mist was so thick that he could touch it; his hand pushed through it, like the webs of a million spiders. Cold. Wetness that slid and clung. Gradually, low to his left, light broke through: a silver disc that showed beyond the ribs of trees: that looked like the moon but was the sun.

Hart shivered. A rime of frost settled on his eyebrows. When Griffiths had ridden in the previous day to see Fredericks there had been signs of it – orange glow of sunlight through shifting, wavering swathes of mist. The night had been the first cold night of fall. And now . . .

Wes Hart wiped a hand across his face and turned towards the barn; he would see to his horse, then eat himself. A shot of whisky in his coffee. Nothing much would be happening a day like this.

He was wrong: it had already happened.

T.C. rode in a couple of hours later, the silver mist clearing, his mount showing every sign of having been driven too hard for too long.

'It's Howie. The bastards shot him.'

He stood there and stared at them – Hart, Fredericks, Peters, Chavez – then pulled his red kerchief from his pocket and broke into a series of coughs which bent him in two, making his thin body shake.

When he looked at them again the red spots were clear on his cheekbones, clear and bright.

'Put three slugs in him. Killed him deader'n a dog.'

Fredericks seized him by the arm. 'Who?'

'The C Circle. Five of 'em.'

'The hell!'

'Where?' demanded Peters, angrily.

'Up at Buffalo. The stage station.'

Hart had already moved away. The rifle lay across the chest in his room, the shotgun was resting on its butt against one side of it. Quickly, without flurry, he picked up each weapon and checked its load. He palmed his Colt and spun the chamber.

He was on his way back down stairs when Fredericks met him, face white with fury. 'They went in to pick up supplies off the stage. Yesterday. Stage came in late and they decided to stop over, head back this morning. C Circle were there spending their money. Drinking. Picked a fight with Howie and T.C. and shot Howie down without a chance. T.C. made a run for it.'

Hart nodded, his face set firm, eyes narrowed.

'The kid, he there?'

Fredericks looked at him. 'Griffiths' boy?'

'Yeah.'

'He was there.'

'Then likely he still is. He won't have gone far in this. Not if he drunk himself stupid last night.'

Hart went to pass Fredericks and the older man grasped his shoulder. 'It doesn't just matter 'cause he was gunned down by five men. It matters 'cause he was workin' for me. And they knew that.'

Hart looked back at him. 'I know it,' he said. 'I know it, too.'

Peters had Hart's horse saddled and ready and Chavez was sitting astride his own mount, a black gelding, toying with his throwing knife.

'You don't have to, you know,' said Hart. 'You ain't paid for it an' I am.'

'I know,' said the Mexican.

Hart turned and looked at Fredericks, who nodded okay.

T.C. sat back against the wall of the house, kerchief held in the three fingers of his left hand, occasionally saying to himself that he should have stayed, he shouldn't have ducked out, Howie was his friend, Howie had been his friend . . .

Hart raised an arm in farewell and spurred the dapple grey mare off into the tatters of mist, the Mexican following.

Buffalo Spring Stage Station was just north of the Unassigned Lands, into the Cherokee Outlet. The main way station building was shaped like a letter L, the longer section sleeping quarters for the Spenglers, who ran the place, and for coach passengers who needed to break the journey. The shorter section was a combination of general store, dining-room and bar. The walls of the station were two logs thick and windows and doors shuttered with planking. Early on the Cheyenne had raided north time after time, mostly taking horses and supplies, once riding off with the Spengler's eldest daughter, a thirteen year old with long fair hair named Martha. It had been after that that Spengler had worked on the fortifications. The Cheyenne had stopped their attacks and he hadn't heard of or seen Martha from that day.

Back of the way station there was a feed barn and at an angle to that a high-fenced corral which held the horses for the stage changeover.

The sun had changed from yellowy-silver through to dull orange by the time Hart and Chavez rode towards the corral, taking their time and keeping their mounts quiet.

Four C Circle stock were in with the other horses.

Chavez and Hart exchanged glances.

'T.C. said five,' Chavez said, pointing.

'I know. Maybe one of 'em slipped away to tell Griffiths.'

'Maybe the son?'

Hart dismounted. 'Maybe.'

They walked towards the door of the way station, Hart with the sawn-off Remington held under the flow of the blue, red and white blanket. His flat-brimmed stetson was angled across the faded blue of his eyes. His right hand brushed the mother-of-pearl grip of his Colt Peacemaker as he moved.

Chavez came a pace behind, sombrero pushed back on his head, rowels of his spurs jingling a little at the back of his patterned leather boots. A Colt Frontier was tied down to his right leg; his long-bladed knife was in a sheath high on his belt, across the left hip.

They were a dozen feet off the door when it opened and a woman came out. Her head and shoulders came out. Hart figured she was Spengler's wife. She stared at the two men for a moment and then her mouth opened in a wordless, warning shout.

Into the sound of her shrill voice came the rapid drum of hoof-beats on hard earth.

As Hart ran for the door he glanced over his shoulder and saw the indistinct shapes of riders approaching fast beyond the corral.

His left shoulder hit the heavy wooden door just as the woman leaned her weight against it, trying desperately to slam it closed. For a second it held and then sprang back. Spengler's wife was hurled back into the room, the door swung hard on its hinges and Hart leaped inside.

Chavez backed in behind him, pistol drawn, watching the approaching men.

Two cowboys, startled awake by the woman's shout, had pushed themselves up from the long table they had been slumped over.

'What the . . .?'

'Hell! Who . . .?'

Hart's right arm blurred and stopped, rock steady. The men choked off their sentences, staring down the barrel of a Colt .45.

Spengler's wife picked herself up from the floor, holding her bruised shoulder and grimacing with discomfort. She began to back off towards the side wall, never taking her eyes from the tall figure in the stetson and Indian blanket.

When she reached the door that led through the wall to the other section of the building, Hart motioned her to stay still. The horses were close now, still coming fast, maybe half a dozen of them.

'It's C Circle!' called Chavez.

One of the cowhands smiled and started to move; Hart stopped him with a glance. Alongside the woman the door opened from the other side and Spengler was standing there, wire-framed spectacles perched on his nose, anxiety in his eyes. Behind him, Hart could see two more men – one of them was Merv Griffiths.

'What shall I do?' called Chavez.

Hart answered without turning his head. 'Shuttin' that damn door might be a good thing.'

Chavez moved inside fast and slammed it shut, slipping the bolts into place and sliding across a wooden beam for extra support.

'You ain't got a chance,' called Merv Griffiths. 'You walked right into it.'

'Shut up!'

Hart jerked the gun towards Spengler. 'Get out of the way.'

The station operator, hesitated, looking at his wife.

'I said get the hell out of the way!'

He moved inside and went to where his wife stood, slipping an arm around her shoulders. Hart could now see that Merv Griffiths had a rifle held low across his body, finger inside the guard and tight against the trigger.

'There's a difference,' said Hart loudly.

'Yeah? What's that?'

'I ain't gettin' caught like Howie.'

Griffiths laughed and started to bring up the rifle; Hart thumbed back the hammer and shot him through the right arm, high and close to the shoulder. The .45 slug screamed through the flesh, gouging an exit wound at the back of the arm. Blood splattered against the wall close by Griffiths and he was hurled after it, the rifle falling from his hands and bouncing along the floor.

One of the C Circle men in the room went for his pistol and Hart flicked aside the blanket and revealed the sawn-off Remington, the twin barrels angled upwards. Both men knew that if Hart fired they would be torn to pieces from such close range.

The cowboy let his gun slip back into its holster.

A shout came from outside: 'What in hell's name's goin' on in there?'

Chavez looked at Hart, who said nothing.

'You want me to get their guns?'

'Sure.'

The man back with Merv Griffiths didn't take to handing over his pistol – until Chavez showed him the keen blade of his knife. Then he changed his mind. Reluctantly, but he changed it.

'You don't open up an' let me in there, we're goin' to break our way in.'

Chavez stacked the guns on the table and stood close by them. Hart motioned with his Colt for Griffiths and the hand by him to come into the room. The sleeve of Merv Griffith's shirt was stained deep with blood and as he walked drops flecked red across the floor. His face was white, the scar showing clearly, blue eyes burning bright as they stared at Hart with hate.

'Get over against that wall!'

The C Circle men moved slowly, casting glances at one another.

Hart passed the shotgun to Chavez. 'If any of 'em breathes too loud let 'em have both barrels. Ain't one of 'em goin' to walk away from that.'

Chavez nodded. 'Where you going?'

'Outside. Talk with that old bull that's doin' all the hollerin'.'

Hart holstered his Colt and went to the door; he called Spengler over. 'Soon as I'm out you shut this behind me. Minute I holler you open it again fast. Don't mess with me.'

Spengler pulled off his spectacles and nodded the air like an old hen pecking for grits. He slipped the wire frames back behind his ears and stood aside.

Hart went out to face the boss of the C Circle.

Griffiths was standing twenty feet away from the way station door. There were three men to his right, two on his left. All six were armed, though only three of them had weapons drawn. Griffiths himself had a pistol holstered high on his right side, the butt above the line of his waist. If he made a play for it, Hart thought, it'd take him an age to clear leather.

'Your boy's in there,' Hart said right out. 'I just put a bullet through his arm.'

For a moment, Griffiths looked as if the slug had gone through himself. The man to the far left levered his Winchester.

'I'm going to finish you for that.' Griffiths voice was grating with scarcely suppressed anger.

Hart shook his head slowly. 'No you ain't.'

'I got enough men here to blast you to hell right now.'

'That ain't what I mean.'

Griffiths stared back at him, not understanding.

Hart took a couple of paces forward. Another shell was levered into another rifle.

'You won't do it 'cause you know he ain't worth killin' for. Not when he's in the wrong like he is.'

Griffiths worked the muscles at the side of his face; his brow furrowed beneath his stetson; the fingers of his right hand pressed against the tooled leather of his holster. Ideas seemed to be struggling behind his grim expression.

'He's my boy,' he said finally, as if that was justification enough, all the cause he needed.

'I know,' said Hart. 'All the more reason for thinkin' what you're doin'. You shoot his way out of this for him an' he's going to carry on down the same road. Every time he feels like actin' mean or stupid he'd goin' to carry on, knowing you'll be by to get him out. That what you want?'

Griffiths looked at Hart a few moments longer, then down at the ground. On either side of him his men waited. No sound came from inside the building.

When Griffiths did speak again, he was quieter, more like a man who had been beaten down in spite of himself. 'Your man died. I don't know if it was Merv or any number of 'em. I'm not even too sure it matters. Only I guess somethin's got to be done.'

'Nothin's goin' to bring Howie back alive. If we hold your boy and anyone else here till a U.S. deputy rides through that might be months off. Even if we could, I don't want to see no man stuck down in them cells at Fort Smith an' not seein' the light of day till he comes up to be stretched at the end of some damn rope.'

'So what you sayin'?'

'Couple of hundred dollars'd get Howie somethin' solid to lie under the ground in. Keep the worms out a mite longer. There'd be plenty to send off to his kin, s'posin' he's got some.'

'And Merv?'

Hart looked at him straight. 'He's your business. You handle him straight an' strong. You don't an' he's goin' to end up with a bullet in him from some lucky drunk in a saloon somewhere between here and Texas.'

Griffiths nodded slowly: Hart stepped back.

'I don't want to kill him,' Hart said. 'Specially not in front of his father.'

Griffiths looked at his men, motioning for them to put up their weapons. 'You want to get him out here?' he asked Hart.

'No. You get him.'

Griffiths sighed and hitched at his belt: 'Okay.'

Hart stood aside and when the rancher was close to the door he yelled for Spengler to open it wide. Griffiths went in and told his men to get their guns and get out. Chavez moved back and watched them carefully, still ready with Hart's shotgun resting on his left arm.

Merv Griffiths went through the door last, sliding his pistol left-handed down into his holster, the beginnings of a smirk playing round the edges of his mouth.

'Thought you was in the saddle, then, didn't you, mister regulator? Well, I knew you wasn't goin' to hold me. You ain't got the balls to . . .'

His father swung his left arm at full stretch and crashed the knuckles of his hand into Merv Griffiths' face. The boy went back on his heels, left leg buckling underneath him. He stared up at his father through an amazement of surprise and pain. Blood seeped between his closed lips.

Griffiths moved round in front of him and waited. When Merv was settled on one knee he looked hard into his face before slapping it again, this time with the flat of his right hand.

The crack echoed round the space in front of the way station.

As Merv went back his left hand swerved towards the butt of his gun. Watching, Hart dived for his own Colt, freeing it from the leather and thumbing back the hammer in a single, smooth movement.

It wasn't necessary.

Griffiths closed fast, stomping his boot down on to his son's left arm and trapping it between heel and sole. Merv stared up at his father, blue eyes flickering. Griffiths ground the edge of the heel hard, leaning his weight down. The boy let the pistol slip from his grasp, opening his mouth in a moan. More blood trickled from the cut corners of his lips.

Griffiths stood away and kicked the gun clear.

'Get up.'

Merv swayed a little and shook his head.

'Get up!'

He glanced up at his father's angry face and pushed down on to the ground, levering himself upwards. Shame etched into his features; he was breathing heavily, audibly.

'I should have done that a long time ago. I don't know when, or why I didn't, but I was wrong. If you put a bullet in that man it's as much my fault as yours.'

Merv Griffiths looked away, past the watching men to the open range, the tops of hills that were still shrouded in mist. His father bent down and picked up the pistol and pushed it down into his own belt. 'Come on,' he said to the rest of his men. 'We're ridin' out.'

Merv stood on the same spot while the C Circle hands mounted up and the first of them began to move away. Hart and Chavez watched him until finally he slowly walked over to his horse and climbed into the saddle, setting off reluctantly in his father's wake.

Hart waited a while, then turned to Chavez. 'Okay. We got us a body to collect. Let's do it.'

Nine

The old man chewed on the quid of dark tobacco, pushing it with his tongue round his almost toothless mouth, letting the juices swell and thicken. When his mouth was to the point of overflowing, he inclined his grizzled head to one side and spat a stream of near black spittle down on to the hard ground.

One of the mules shifted nervously, pricking back its ears. The old man eased himself forward from his place against the wagon wheel and pulled the Winchester over towards him.

A shape broke the skyline: horse and rider.

He levered a shell into the chamber and settled back, working the cud with a little more energy than before. So much of his time was passed alone, he was more than likely to welcome someone in the way of company. Thing was, out in the Territory there was no way of knowing who might ride in on you. What they might want.

The rider was coming in good and slow, taking his own time. The old man looked at him from under the bent brim of his hat, taking in the tall shape and the flat-crowned stetson, the wash of colour from the blanket draped about the rider as it swayed with the movements of the grey horse.

'Howdy!'

Pulling in his mount, Wes Hart looped the reins round the saddle pommel and swung down to the ground.

'You sure do travel some.'

The old man nodded: 'Man has the need.' He spat a squirt of tobacco juice out of the corner of his mouth, the ends of it dribbling down his chin and curling on to his neck. He ignored it, letting it run. 'Some men,' he added.

'Uh-huh.' Hart glanced at the wagon. 'You got any whisky in there?'

'For the right price I got most things.'

'Whisky'll do. Help keep back the cold.'

The old man got up slowly, his left leg making a noticeable creaking noise when he put pressure on it. He went slowly round to the back of the wagon, favouring his left side. The whisky was in a labelless bottle and looked the colour of cat's piss.

Hart pulled the cork free with his teeth and had a quick swallow; he jerked the bottle away from his face like it had bitten him.

'Jesus! Where the hell you get this stuff?'

'Down on the Texas border.' He chuckled. 'No one ever complained about it afore.'

'Then that's 'cause it ripped their tongues clear out.'

The old man chuckled some more, slavering at the mouth. 'Take the weight of your legs for a while.'

Hart nodded and sat down, closing his eyes and grimacing as he gave himself another shot of the whisky. He offered the bottle to the trader, who shook his head and carried on chomping on his tobacco.

'Hear you're workin' for Fredericks.'

'That's right.'

'Regulator.'

'Yeah.'

The old man spat out more juice, then broke into a fit of coughing.

'How d'you like the job?' he said when he recovered.

'It pays.'

'Uh-huh.' The trader wiped the sleeve of his coat across his mouth.

'An' Fredericks?'

Hart hesitated. 'He ain't the kind of man I'd choose to ride with.'

The old timer reached out his hand. 'P'raps I will take me a swig of that – seein' as you've paid for it.'

Hart passed across the bottle.

'Met a feller name of Probert. You know him?'

Hart nodded. 'Indian agent up at the Cheyenne Nation. That him?'

'That's the one.'

The old man half-choked on the whisky and passed the bottle back.

Hart waited for the trader to come out with whatever he was leading up to; he sure wasn't a man to fall over his words in a hurry.

'Got speakin' with him an' he told me 'bout a deal him an' Fredericks cooked up with the Cheyenne for grazin' rights. Didn't come right out with it, but seems he an' Fredericks worked it pretty close to their chests.'

'I know that.'

'Said somethin' else you might not know. Fredericks asked Probert to let him see his government report. Wanted to add a few things of his own. Offered Probert enough money to make it worth his while.'

Hart sat forward. 'What kind of things?'

'Far as I could tell, stuff 'bout Indian raids an' such. Wanted Probert to play it up enough so's he could holler for the army to come into the Territory.'

'The army! What in hell's name he want them in here for?'

The old man shrugged: 'Search me. If Probert knew, he weren't sayin'.'

Hart got up and pushed the cork down into his bottle. 'Thanks, anyway. Maybe I'll have words with Fredericks, see what he's got to say.'

'Suit yourself.' The trader spat sideways. 'Watch him, though. I reckon he's slippery as a salmon in flood tide.'

Hart pushed the bottle down into his saddle bag and climbed aboard the grey. 'I'll do that. Be seein' you.'

The old man raised a hand and leaned back against the wagon wheel to watch Hart ride away towards the north-west. Before long he was having difficulty in picking out the shapes of man and horse from the shifting grass and the encroaching hills.

The carbine shots came close together, three of them, breaking the cold stillness of the sky. Hart reined in and looked off to the right, in the direction from which the firing had come. The land rose up into a humped hill which seemed to split narrowly near its summit.

'C'mon, Clay.'

Freeing his own rifle from its scabbard as he rode, Hart spurred his horse towards the hill, echoes of the three shots fading about him.

As he neared the head of the hill he could see that the ground split away into a jagged fissure which opened gradually as it descended. Midway down, a stream sprang out from the ground and ran down towards the valley. A sprawl of small cottonwoods littered either side of the water. To the right of these he could see Peters, his horse hobbled and grazing fifteen yards behind.

Peters was kneeling beside the body of a calf, his carbine resting against his leg. A small fire was smouldering close by.

Hart called out clear, making sure Peters knew who he was, then rode the grey mare carefully down, crossing and re-crossing the steep contours of the slope.

The calf was roped, its head moving in fear, damp brown eyes large and soft. The chestnut hide on its flank was singed by the C Circle brand.

'They was fixin' to alter the brand when I spotted 'em. Lit out down the valley.' Peters pointed west.

'One calf,' said Hart. 'Don't make a lot of sense.'

'I know it.'

Peters reached for the knife sheathed at the back of his belt and severed the rope. The animal held still a couple of seconds then scrambled up and ran unsteadily away. Fifteen yards on it stopped and pushed head and neck forward, letting out an anguished cry for its mother.

Peters straightened up, hefting the carbine across his chest. 'Didn't get too good a look, but they seemed like kids. Three of 'em.'

He shook his head and scratched at one side of his drooping moustache. 'They'll be comin' in here an' runnin' off cattle like this all the time. I don't know what the hell Fredericks reckoned you was goin' to do about it. Not one man. However good you are with that fancy gun you tote round. Nothin' 'cept a whole bunch of deputies goin' to clear all the rustlers an' damn renegade Indians off this range. Less'n it's the goddamn army.'

Hart looked at the top hand keenly, trying to figure out if he knew anything more than he was likely to let on. But Peters turned away and began to walk over towards his horse. Hart kicked his boot through the ashes of the fire.

'Which way you headed?'

Peters pushed his greasy stetson forward on his head. 'Got a couple of new hands comin' in. Lazy J herd's through in a couple of days. Want to show 'em the range.'

'Okay. I'll see what I can pick out followin' this trail down the valley.'

Peters swung his horse away without another word and moved towards the northern slope. Hart clicked his tongue against the roof of his mouth and shook the reins; the grey started into a walk. A way past the calf, it let out another braying cry and broke into an uneven trot, following Hart between the cottonwoods.

The three rustlers had left a clear trail, one of their mounts without a shoe on his rear right side and beginning to limp. The trees thinned out to nothing and the valley broadened; the sun was pale and filtered through streaks of grey cloud; the wind blew strongly into Hart's face. He pulled the brim of his hat down over his eyes and carried on.

Another couple of miles and he came upon the lame horse. They'd pulled the saddle clear and left it to hobble painfully until it fell and didn't get up. By that time birds of prey would have begun to gather blackly in the sky, circling.

Hart pulled the Henry from its scabbard and lifted the stock towards his shoulder, guiding Clay with his knees and feet. For an instant the abandoned horse looked at him balefully; the shot cracked out like the sudden breaking of bone. Hart looked back the way he had come – in the distance he could see the shape of the calf, straggled and lost.

He pushed the barrel of the rifle back inside its sheath and let it slide home. Then, pulling on his horse's reins, he started to canter along the trail.

The country became more broken, beginnings of hills that fell back to nothing, outbreaks of brush, bare-branched trees.

Hart dropped from his saddle and examined the tracks carefully. He guessed they knew he was following them now and were driving ahead as fast as they could. But with one horse being ridden double, they were in difficulties.

Hart nodded to himself, remounted and rode wide of the trail, circling to the south.

Kevin and Danny Caughie were cousins. Their folks had come out to Kansas when the boys were around ten and eleven and tried to make a go of it as farmers. By the time they were fourteen and fifteen it had been clear to them that their folks weren't going to make it. They'd laid by a few supplies over a week or so and then one night they'd sneaked into the larder and taken as much as they could. Kevin's pa had caught them midway between the house and the barn. In sheer fright Kevin had thrown a sack of flour at his father, hitting him in the face and knocking him down. Danny had jumped on him and started striking him about the head with the butt of an old pistol. He might even have fired it, except that he didn't have any shells and the mechanism didn't work any longer.

Kevin pulled him away, his father's scalp a bloodied mess of hair and torn skin, and the two of them ran to the barn and took horses.

Less than a week later they met up with Lon. That was the only name he acknowledged, the only name he went by. Whenever either of the cousins asked him about his folks or where he came from, Lon would give them a warning look that shut them up till the next time their curiosity threatened to overcome them.

Lon was a couple of years older and had a Colt Frontier that he claimed to have taken single-handed from a deputy sheriff in north Kansas. Neither Kevin nor Danny said anything to doubt it.

It was Lon who said they should ride down into the Indian Territories. Rustling down there was easy, he assured them. There wasn't no law to speak of. They could cut out steers just as they liked.

To Kevin and Danny it had sounded good. Better than watching year after year of dying, fading crops and thinning, emaciated milk cows. Better than chewing on the sleeve of your coat to bite back the overwhelming hunger.

Now, with Danny astride the rump of Kevin's horse, his saddle heavy on his own back, bumping against it as they rode, neither of them were so sure. Somewhere behind them, someone was coming after them and no matter how much Lon might curse and tell them if the no-good bastard was unlucky enough to catch up with them he'd earn a slug in his belly, they were scared.

Suddenly there was a movement through the line of trees to the left and a mounted man broke cover less than twenty yards ahead.

'Hold it there!'

Kevin nearly lost the reins, trying to haul them in. Lon cursed and swerved his horse to one side. The man had a hat low over his face and an Indian blanket draped from his right shoulder. A sawn-off shotgun was steady in his right hand, angled over the neck of the dapple grey he was riding.

'Jesus!'

Danny let go his grip on the saddle and it fell awkwardly behind him. Lon swung his horse sideways, trying to manoeuvre himself so that he could make a move for his pistol without being seen.

Kevin stared, open-mouthed, seeing the barrels of the shotgun discharging into him, blasting him apart.

'You'll be dead, boy! Do it and you'll be dead.'

Lon turned his head angrily, but he kept his hand where it lay, on the butt of the gun, not pulling it clear. Hart ignored the other two and edged his horse closer. The grey threw back her head and let out a snicker. Lon eased the gun a couple of inches.

'I mean it.'

Kevin and Danny were staring at him, half wanting him to go through with the draw, half hoping that he wouldn't. Once bullets began to fly they could see themselves ending up dead.

'Get down and keep your right hand high all the way.'

Lon scowled, not wanting to lose face in front of the others. But the Remington was awful close, too close.

'Now lift it out with your left hand, finger and thumb.'

Lon did as he was told, picking the gun from the holster and holding it out in front of his body.

'Toss it over here.'

Lon scowled again, hesitated, threw the pistol through a looping curve so that it bounced on the end of the barrel and came to rest on its side between himself and Hart.

'Now back off, boy,'

Lon went back a couple of paces and Hart moved towards the gun. As he stooped to scoop it up, Lon charged, head down shoulders thrust forward, coming like a young bull. He was fast – so fast that Kevin and Danny thought he might make it.

Hart arched his body backwards and swung the shotgun round on its trigger guard. His right arm went up and as Lon came in hard underneath its swing, he brought the stock of the weapon down into the side of his head. The heavy wood smashed against Lon's cheekbone, splintering it beneath the skin. The skin itself broke back like a flower peeling into bloom. Blood ran down his face and on to his neck. He hit the ground with a thump and rolled over; tried to push himself back to his feet and failed, falling away again.

Hart grabbed him by the front of his shirt and hauled him to his feet. He shook him like an angry dog shakes a rabbit.

'I knew it. I knew you weren't goin' to listen to reason without I gave you a good beating.'

Lon winced as the pain from the side of his face shot through him. He was breathing heavily, open-mouthed, blood was still trickling from the torn skin.

'You ain't ... you ain't ... tellin' me nothin' ... who you think ... you are ... ain't no law ... anythin' ...'

Hart looked at the boy with a hint of despair in his eyes; still holding him with his left hand he hit him with his right, the fist bunched hard. Lon's head jerked back and his eyes closed fast, arms dropping away at either side. Hart let him go and he toppled down in a mess of arms and legs, near shapeless.

Hart turned to the other two.

'How many head you changed brands on round here?'

'N ...' Kevin began, then floundered.

'None.' Blurted Danny. 'We was just fixin' that calf when someone happened along. We lit out. That was all.'

His dark eyes spoke the truth of what he'd said.

'Land either side of Turkey Creek belongs to Fredericks. That makes it my responsibility. I catch sight of any of you boys again I'm not going to be usin' the butt end of this.' He lifted up the shotgun and patted its twin barrels with his other hand. 'You sure you understand that?'

'Yes . . .'

'We got it. Honest, mister. We won't even stay round these parts. We'll . . .'

Hart waved him silent. 'Okay. When he wakes up, you see he understand the same. An' if he's too stubborn to see sense, you pair keep movin', you understand me? Get down as far as Fort Reno, you might find some sort of work, stables or somethin'.'

Danny nodded his head; Kevin gulped and mumbled thanks. On the ground, Lon still hadn't budged. Hart went over to his horse and mounted up, sliding the shotgun down into its special saddle holster. He gave the boys a final warning glance then turned the grey towards the east.

Moving ahead of him, in his mind's eye, was the slender figure of a fourteen year old sitting astride an old plough horse, blue eyes still bright and not yet faded by twenty years of living.

Ten

'While you were tanning a few fool kids, fifty head of cattle were being run off north of here. You understand what I'm saying? Fifty head! While you were wasting your time over one miserable calf.'

The words resonated round the room. Fredericks stood upright, his breath coming noisily through his nostrils, cheeks florid and lips white with anger.

His fist struck the table. 'You understand me?'

Hart stared back at him unflinching: 'Sure I understand you.'

'Then what the hell you got to say about it?'

'Nothing.'

'Nothing! What kind of answer is that? Fifty head of cattle rustled and you got nothing to say about it.'

'Talkin' won't get 'em back.'

Fredericks rubbed the knuckles of his right hand inside his left. 'Oh, you do intend to get them back?'

'What do you think?'

'I was beginning to wonder. I thought perhaps you weren't so hot at tackling grown men as you like to make out.'

Hart's eyes narrowed and he flexed the fingers of his right hand. Fredericks saw the movement and wondered if he had gone too far. His own hand moved towards his coat pocket where he kept the derringer.

'T.C. reckoned he knew which way they was headed, didn't he?'

Fredericks released a pent-up breath, stilled his hand. 'Yes.'

The map was rolled up in the centre of the table; Fredericks pulled it out, holding down one corner while Hart kept the other side from flapping back.

'He said they drove them east, this trail along here.'

Fredericks traced a path with his finger, moving away from Turkey Creek across the Cherokee Outlet, over in the direction of Stillwater. A range of hills pushed up between.

Hart looked at the map, not so much at what Fredericks was showing him, but at a series of dotted red lines that had been carefully drawn in.

'What are these?'

'What?' Fredericks leaned back, looking across at Hart.

The lines went east and south, encircling a wide area of the Unassigned Lands and the Outlet, reaching as far over as area occupied by the Pawnees.

'They must be there for somethin'. You wasn't just doodlin' when you put those little bits of red ink round that land.'

Fredericks went round the table, pulling at the bottom of his coat, the cuff of his sleeve. 'There's room for a man to carve out for himself one of the biggest spreads in the whole frontier. By the time this territory gets statehood, whoever that is is going to be in a pretty powerful position.'

Hart looked at him with a trace of amusement. 'And that someone's going to be you?'

'Why not?' Fredericks moved again, away from the table and towards the window. He paused for a moment and leaned against the glass, peering down. When he turned away his breath had left a misted smear on the pane.

'It needs a man of vision to get this territory on its feet. Someone to get hold of it by the scruff of the neck and shake it into shape.' Fredericks' face was flushed with excitement; his voice loud and growing louder. Both hands were clasped tightly before him.

'We need to impress law and order on it. Stamp down hard.'

'Clear the Indians out?' asked Hart, interrupting.

Fredericks coughed, adjusted his tie. 'I didn't say that.'

'Settlers, then? Sodbusters? Small ranchers?'

Fredericks shrugged, irritated.

'Someone's got to move out so that you can, what was it? Carve out one of the biggest spreads on the frontier?'

'There's hundreds of miles of open range . . .'

'An' these damned settlers dropped all over it – not to mention the Indians.'

Fredericks went back to the table and began to roll up the map; Hart jabbed a finger down and kept it where it was. Around Stillwater.

'How were you plannin' to get this land? Just take it?'

'It's free land.'

Fredericks' eyes, beginning to turn watery, a skein of dull yellow showing below one pupil.

'And the people already on it?'

'Why does it matter?'

'Because it does.'

Fredericks held his breath then exhaled slowly: it carried the smell of whisky strongly.

'They'll be made an offer. A fair one.'

Hart let his finger slip off the edge of the map and it sprang back together and rolled a little.

'Will be or have been already?'

'I don't see . . .'

Hart's hand was on Fredericks' arm before he realized what was happening; the grip wasn't strong, almost gentle; the tone of his voice was soft. Still there was no mistaking the menace in Hart's manner. Fredericks didn't understand why Hart was so interested, why he was interested at all. But he didn't like the way things were going. Not for the first first time he wondered at the wisdom of taking Hart on as regulator. If it would be justified by the uses he was putting it to.

'You've already made an offer.' It was no longer a question.

'Yes.'

'How long ago?'

'Not long. Weeks.'

Hart released Fredericks' arm and automatically Fredericks brushed his hand down the sleeve.

'You satisfied now?'

Hart gave a wry smile and backed away from the table. 'I'll likely be away a couple of days. Maybe three.'

At the door, he turned his head. 'Those new guns you gave to them Cheyenne who came with the agent. Sign of good faith, I suppose you'd call it. You wouldn't have been handing them out in greater numbers than that, would you?'

For a second, Fredericks hesitated, taken aback. Then he did his favourite trick of thumping the table with his fist. 'That's a damn fool question! Do you think I'd run the risk of letting large numbers of guns get into the hands of mindless savages like that? What sort of fool d'you take me for?'

Hart smiled and turned away. He answered the question to the wrong side of the door. 'A clever one,' he said. 'A clever one.'

*

The grass became shorter, tougher; patches of reddish earth poked through. The first oaks tracked along the creek flowing like silver from the north-east. Hart pulled his gloved hands back on the reins. A black bird crawked its way from their midst with a glint of light-coloured beak as it passed across the dipping sun.

The cattle were grazing on the far side of the slope, straggling out into a thinning line to the north. Around fifty head. At the creek edge a group of half a dozen, detached from the rest, drank lazily. Hart let the grey move forward a few yards and one steer lifted up its head from the water and turned as if to face him, long horns cleaving the cold air.

Hart steadied the mare; the steer went back to its drinking.

There was no one apparently watching over the cattle. Hart didn't like that; he didn't understand it. He touched his spurs to the grey's flanks and started to move carefully forward, edging down in the direction of the creek.

When they reached the water, the horse dipped its head to drink and Hart loosed his grip on the reins. The cattle were maybe a hundred and fifty yards away. Stars glimmered on the ridges of running water as their movements caught the sun.

'C'mon, Clay.'

The words were so soft that at first the mare didn't seem to have heard them. When she shook her head, drops of moisture fell away.

'C'mon.'

Ten yards past the creek, a sudden gust of wind shifted Hart's stetson on his head. As he turned his face away from the wind he realized why no one was watching the cattle – they were watching him instead.

Two men close together, mounted, on the hill from which he had first seen the rustled steers. A third man further round, closer to the trees.

Hart stopped his horse, tongue pushing his upper lip. He could make a break for it – Clay would likely be able to outrun any of their mounts with ease. He could turn and wade into them, drop one, maybe two before much shooting got underway.

First one, then a second and a third of the men slipped their rifles from beside their saddles.

'You ain't plannin' on stealing them cows, are you?'

At first he didn't recognize the voice, not really until she rode out from between two oaks and even then he had the wild idea that it was Fredericks' wife involved in some absurd plan against her husband. But nothing about them was the same – and when she spoke a second time, Hart knew full well who she was.

' 'Cause if you are we just might have to take you up the hill an' let you swing in the wind a little.'

Belle Starr was wearing dark green pants cut from velvet and a light green shirt that might have been silk. Over that she wore a wool vest without sleeves and a gun belt across her breasts. She had on shiny boots and a brown hat with a single feather sticking from the band. As usual Belle rode side-saddle, a riding crop hanging from her wrist.

Her face was strong, handsome rather than beautiful.

When she opened her mouth her teeth showed stained and uneven.

'That was what you did for them two you picked off from the gang, wasn't it. One of 'em no more than a fool kid. You flashed your deputy badge an' that Colt of yours an' run 'em off to Fort Smith so's that bastard Parker could add two more to his list.' She spat at the ground. 'Murderous bastard!'

Hart sighed. 'Belle, I didn't like that any more'n you did.'

'Maybe. You did it, though, didn't you?'

'Yeah, an' I throwed in my badge after.'

Belle snorted: 'After! Well, Jesus Christ, I sure hope them two poor strangled bastards appreciated the sacrifice you made.'

She let her horse come right up to Clay, looking into Hart's face with a mixture of pride and contempt and something that was less easy to define.

'Venus!'

She reined in the mare when the two animals were head to head. Hart was close enough to be able to reach out and touch her. Close enough to smell her body.

'It was you let me take 'em.'

'I knew you'd throw that in my face sometime.' She glared at him, the riding crop slapping against the polished leather of her boot. 'You think I didn't recall that when I heard how they went – how long it took that kid to die?'

Her eyes burned into him.

'And now?' he asked.

She pulled away a little. 'You heard what I said. I want to know what you're doin' sniffin' round these cattle.'

'I ain't about to change their brands, that's for sure.'

'Meanin'?'

Hart pulled his horse away, wheeling it round in a tight circle. One of the men on the hill let his mount ride down some twenty yards, bringing his rifle close to his shoulder.

'Don't waste times playin' games with me, Belle. These steers are here 'cause you rustled 'em.'

'And you?' She came towards him again, the outline of her breasts clear against her shirt, nipples hard and cold.

'I'm workin' for Fredericks.'

The side of her mouth twitched sharply, making her face suddenly ugly. He could smell her body again: flesh that he had never touched.

'Regulator?'

Hart nodded, glancing beyond her at the three men on the hill – a second had moved now, coming round as if to circle the valley.

'I asked you this once before . . .' Belle Starr's voice was softer; she moved a hand till it touched, for a second, his leg. '. . . you aimin' to do anythin' 'bout you an' me?'

Hart's eyes held hers for several moments. He wanted her: there, then; in the cold; in the trees.

'No, Belle,' he said.

She raised her riding crop fast and brought it slashing down against his right arm; pain bit through him and he swayed sideways in the saddle. She used the crop again, but this time on the black mare. The instant she had cleared him, two rifle shots ploughed the ground close by the legs of Hart's horse.

Belle Starr shouted something he couldn't make out. He drew his gun fast, wincing as the movement took up the blow with the riding crop. A third rifle shot whistled close to his head and he fired three times himself, firing fast, quick, covering shots, then rocking his body, kicking with his boots, moving Clay towards the anxious cattle.

The longhorns were pawing the ground, heads lifted on the air, beginning to push against each other. Hart fired twice over them, shouting, waving his stetson with his left hand.

More rifle shots cracked out and Hart could hear the sound of galloping hoofs. Useless to turn round. The cattle were moving now, bellowing, gathering speed, racing down the creek valley.

Hart manoeuvred Clay between the hind-runners, yelling at them to clear the way, knowing the danger of riding in the midst of the stampeding animals but realizing that the other, following, danger was the greater.

The noise of the cattle was almost overwhelming. Hart stopped flailing his arm and leaned low over Clay's neck, urging every ounce of speed from the mare. As shots still tried to pick him off, he broke through the front of the steers and sensed the horse beneath him finding fresh energies now that they were not so tightly surrounded.

Hart veered right, making for the tree line, now allowing himself to glance over his shoulder. Two of the men were still coming, the third was sitting astride his mount a quarter of a mile back, the animal's head lowered to the ground. Further back was a small, dark shape he took to be Belle Starr.

As he reached the first oaks, Hart reined in the mare and swung round, pulling the Henry from its scabbard. He thumbed up the rear sight on the stock, worked the lever. Realizing what was happening, the two chasing men spread wide. Hart moved the rifle barrel marginally and squeezed back on the trigger. The horse of the nearest rider stopped as if it had raced into an invisible wall. Front legs splayed, dipped; the body began to fall even as the man was hurled, somersaulting, forwards.

His companion turned his mount away, galloping back down in the direction of the creek. Hart let the rifle drop down into its sheath and moved Clay about, passing between the trees.

Eleven

Like a lot of sod houses, it had been built into the overhang of a hill, back wall formed from the solid ground. A lean-to at the far side was missing several planks completely, others had slipped from place, become broken. Nobody had bothered to repair or replace them.

In the muted brightness of the moonlight, the manes of horses shone dully as they moved restlessly in the corral. The man sitting on the end of the fence turned his head a little, pulled his collar up against the cold and tucked his head back down inside it. It was a bastard of a night to draw guard!

The others in there, drinking raw whisky and playing some cards, likely draw poker. Warmth of the stove. Later Belle and Sam would get into their cot behind the curtain and they'd be goin' at it half the night, not giving a damn about who heard them. The rest of the boys in their blankets on the floor trying not to notice how hard they were getting, listening to that woman's moans and growls of pleasure.

Jesus Almighty!

She weren't no raving beauty but there was something about the way she looked at a man, some special way of eyeing him that let you know she could treat you like no woman ever did before or would after. And you didn't even have to see her; it was enough to be close to her – scent of her body, sweat and skin strong inside a man's head.

The guard pushed up his head and turned left and then right. What in hell's name was spooking those horses he didn't know. God, he wished a little light would start to show; he wished it would be morning.

He felt it before his eyes registered anything; hard and sharp against his throat. Mouth opening, he saw the shape close – from nowhere – choking, he felt it push alongside the windpipe, thrusting against his neck. Blood filled his mouth. A face moved fast in front of his own, one he couldn't recognize, see clearly. He knew he was falling forwards and that an arm was catching him; he was folding over it. He spewed vomit and blood from his opened mouth. His neck burnt like fire. The knife slid out of his body. He didn't know if he was lying down or still falling; didn't know if his eyes were open or closed; didn't know . . .

Wes Hart bent down and wiped the razor-sharp blade of the Apache knife on the man's coat sleeve and then stood back up. He dropped the knife down into the sheath hanging from a cord round his neck and pushed it down between shirt and skin.

Light seeped through the sacking tacked over the windows; smoke rolled out from the hole in the roof above the stove.

Hart moved silently back to where he had tied Clay, by the far side of the corral. He lifted the shotgun from its holster and broke it, checking the load. Stealthily back again towards the door.

Outside he transferred the Remington to his left hand and drew the Colt .45. He guessed there would be a bolt pushed to behind the door, possibly a length of wood slotted into place. He stood one pace back – if the kick didn't work he would use the shotgun and blast the timber apart.

A cloud shut across the moon.

Hart lifted his right leg and rammed the underneath of his boot flat against the wood, closest to the handle. The door rocked and sprang open. Hart jumped through before it had struck the wall.

'Hold it!'

Belle Starr was standing at the rear of the single room, close by the stove. Surprise startled her dark eyes. Sam was sitting at the head of the rough wooden table, cleaning a pistol. Three others were sitting around the other end, playing cards. The dealer held his action in mid-flow; slowly one card slipped away from his fingers and fluttered to the table top.

'You're a fool!' the words hissed through Belle's tight lips.

Hart shook his head, holding both guns steady. The shotgun was covering the card players, the Colt aimed at the centre of Sam's chest.

'Get to your feet. One at a time an' slow. Take your gun out with your other hand an' get over by the wall.'

He jerked the shotgun barrel at the dealer.

'You. First.'

The man blanched and scraped back his chair, never taking his eyes off the weapon in Hart's left hand. He stood up slowly and reached his left hand across to his holster.

'Finger and thumb.'

The man nodded, jaw hanging down some on his lean face. Sam Starr fidgeted on his chair and Hart flicked his eyes in his direction. Finger and thumb were on the pistol butt. The man at the end of the table kicked his chair backwards and threw himself to the floor, grabbing at his gun. Sam tried to turn the table but it was too heavy and only rocked. The dealer moved his hand down on to his pistol and started his draw.

Hart squeezed back on the shotgun, arching his body backwards as he did so. The dealer was lifted from the ground and hurled through the air, crashing into the solid wall. His face simply ceased to exist; instead there was a bloody pulp that denied any shape. The upper part of his chest was raked throught with shot.

Hart swung the Colt away from Sam towards the man who'd dived for the floor. As the man's pistol came up from its holster, Hart fired the Colt twice. The first shot shattered the bone below the neck and deflected upwards along the side of his head, tearing away his left ear. The second slug hammered through his chest and he arched up under its impact, eyes closing, fingers splaying wide, the gun falling away.

Belle Starr had jumped in front of the body of the shotgunned man, her gun belt hanging from the back of a chair in the corner.

'Don't, Belle!'

Hart thumbed back the hammer on his Colt as Sam stood up and lifted his own chair into the air, aiming it towards the kerosene lantern hanging from the ceiling.

Belle Starr pulled the .36 Manhattan clear and started to turn. The third of the card players dived low into Hart's body. Sam smashed his chair into the lantern, sending it to the floor.

There was a sudden flare and then the light was all but gone. Just the dull glow from the stove. A shot rang out and Hart felt something graze his left arm, inches above the elbow. Arms were tight around his legs, trying to force him over. He fired the Colt and heard the bullet whine away harmlessly.

An arm swung near him and a chair back shattered against his head.

He went down heavily, the man who'd been pulling at his legs releasing his grip and trying to scramble over him. A boot rammed down into his stomach and he opened his mouth in a shout. Two more shots were fired harmlessly in the room.

Sam Starr was yelling for Belle to come after him, to make a run for it. Hart rolled sideways and pushed himself to his feet. He could see Belle still near the back of the room, hear Sam still shouting, the voice receding.

He scrabbled on the floor for the Colt that had got knocked from his hand.

Belle made nó move: waited.

Outside, the sound of horses being led from the corral. Hart found the Colt and jumped through the doorway. A couple of shots sent him low to the side, stopping him. One man was already mounted, leading a horse for the second. Another shot came from the man on the horse and then as the other one jumped for the saddle, Hart snapped off a shot and started to run.

Clay was twenty-five yards back; dapple grey coat showing in the moonlight. Hart freed her reins and slapped her flank, one hand grasping the saddle pommel.

The pair had got a start but not one that the grey couldn't make up. The earth was hard and black beneath her hoofs. Hart leaned forward in the saddle, urging her along, looking for the riders he could hear up ahead.

As the land slanted upwards and the trail broke between two groups of brush he saw them, riding one behind the other, going at full gallop. The moon showed them in strong silhouette as they hit the top of the slope. Hart though of stopping and using the Henry but before he could decide they had dropped down from sight on the other side.

'Clay! C'mon! Let's go!'

Hart's voice was loud in the clearness of the night; the drum of hoofs reverberated from the hard ground.

He could see them clearly as he raced down the far slope, closing fast with them now. Anxiously, first one then the other of them glanced back over their shoulders. Hart touched his hand to the stock of the rifle, reins tight in his grasp.

Yards shortened between them.

The rider at the back wheeled off the trail to the right and started to turn back to face Hart, pulling his own pistol clear. Hart thought, made the decision, hauled hard on the reins. As Clay slowed and swung round, he heard the first shot and levered a shell into the chamber of the Henry.

The man was coming directly at him and he brought the rifle to his shoulder. It would have to be a lucky shot with a pistol travelling at that speed. His eye squinted along the sight at the dark shape, squeezed the trigger once, brought the gun down, worked the lever a second time.

Unnecessary.

The man spread his arms wide and rocked back in the saddle, feet coming out of the stirrups. As the horse continued on its way, the man fell to the ground and rolled several times. The riderless animal veered wide, out of Hart's path.

Hart sent Clay forward at a walk, keeping the rifle at the ready in case.

He lay with one arm high above his head, the other twisted up behind his back as though it had been broken in the fall. His legs were spread from the knees. The bullet had punched an entry wound inches wide in his left side, midway up the chest. Hart turned him on to his side, using his boot. The broken arm flopped awkwardly – there was no other movement.

It wasn't Sam Starr.

Hart shrugged and turned away. Back by his horse, he reloaded his guns before remounting. The shotgun was back at the place the gang had been using for a hideout and he intended to ride back for it. After that he guessed he'd get back to the Fredericks' place.

There wasn't any point in lighting out after Sam now and Belle would be clear away.

He went back easily, letting the grey pick her own pace. The door to the sod house was still wide open and there were traces of fire still showing from the stove. The shotgun had been knocked well into the room during the struggle and lay on the floor beyond the table.

Hart bent to pick it up and heard the noise at the door. He spun fast, right hand diving for the butt of the Colt and pulling it clear from the greased holster, thumbing the hammer, finger beginning to work the trigger.

He was crouched low, left arm put wide for balance. Belle Starr stood in the doorway, the .36 tight in her gloved hand and aimed right at Hart's chest.

The moment froze time. Their eyes caught. Neither fired.

'I didn't think you'd be here.'

'Of course you didn't.' Belle's eyes seemed black in the half-light.

Hart straightened up, hand steady on the gun, the barrel still pointing at Belle's left breast.

'Sam?' she asked.

Hart shook his head. 'He rode clear.'

'And Jed?'

'If that's what he was called, he's dead.'

She blinked for a moment, letting her body relax. Slowly she lowered her gun, letting her arm fall by her side. Hart released the hammer of the Colt .45.

Apart from that neither of them moved. The bodies of two of her gang were where they'd fallen.

'What now?' Hart asked.

She gave a half smile. 'I'm going after Sam.'

Hart nodded and then said: 'Why?'

For a few seconds she seemed to think about it.

'Because . . .'

'He ran out an' left you.'

'Sam knew I'd make it on my own.'

'Maybe you won't always, Belle.'

She frowned. 'Some day, perhaps. Could be that's why I'm goin' after Sam and not stayin' round here.'

'You're keepin' clear of Fredericks' range?'

Belle took half a pace inside the room. 'If I don't then sooner or later one of us is goin' to put a bullet through the other. I don't want that to happen.'

'Me neither.'

Hart went close to her and for a moment he thought about taking her in his arms. But it would have been starting something neither of them would have been able to handle.

'You're not going to stop me?' She looked up into his face.

Hart shook his head.

'Okay.' She lay her hand on his arm and the warmth of it sent a shiver to his brain. Again he could smell her.

She stopped outside the doorway and turned. 'Some feller at Fort Reno – whatever you done to him got him plenty riled.'

'How's that?'

'Enough to offer good money to get you killed.'

Hart went cold; he remembered the rifle shots from the trees by the Peterson place, the attempt by the ferryman to gun him down.

'Who was it, Belle?'

'Didn't know his name. Youngish feller, late twenties. Good-lookin' in a empty sort of way. Sort of sandy hair.' She looked at Hart with a grudging smile. 'He hates you worse than poison.'

'He say why?'

'Not to me he didn't. But then I wasn't interested in takin' him up on his offer.'

'Yeah. Well, thanks for the warnin', Belle.'

She nodded, her head for a moment angled to one side. Velvet was waiting alongside the lean-to.

'Maybe we'll meet again, Wes,' she said from the saddle. 'But I doubt it.'

Hart stepped forward and raised his hand.

It was time to head back towards the Fredericks place. There were questions which still needed to be answered, which had to be asked. Soon the shape of woman and horse were no more than a greater dark against the land and sky, then not that. Hoofbeats faded. Hart was thinking back to the time he'd ridden by the

Peterson place in the early morning and seen Carol standing with her arm about her husband. He recalled the man's clean-shaven, open face, his sandy hair.

Twelve

The little girl was running, aimlessly, legs always threatening to give way under her as she stumbled, recovered, stumbled again. At the hill crest she was swallowed up in the brightness of the rising sun, disappearing as if the strength of its heat had consumed her. Then she was there at the other side, a glow tracing the outline of her skin.

Hart had heard the shooting several miles off and driven the dapple grey at a gallop. Now he veered to the right, moving fast towards the girl.

She saw him coming, panicked and tried to run faster. With a cry she fell headlong; picked herself up and began to run again. The horse came close by her and Hart leaned sideways from the saddle, scooping her up in his arm.

She struggled frantically, shouting and swinging her arms, kicking with her legs. He sat her across the front of the saddle and her bunched little fists struck at his chest again and again.

Hart reined in the horse and held her with both hands; when she could hit him no longer the tears ran down her face and her mouth gulped in gouts of air. The hair on her head, cut to the scalp because of nits or some such, had begun to grow slowly, unevenly.

Shots still sounded from the other side of the hill.

'Listen, you stay here. You'll be okay. I'll go and help your folk.'

She didn't hear him; eyes clenched tight, the crying continued unabated.

'Stay here. You'll be all right.'

He shook her, trying to get her to look at him, to understand what he was saying. Fear gripped her totally. Finally, Hart lifted her round and set her down on the ground. Then she did look at him and for a few moments the crying ceased, though her body heaved with soundless sobs.

'Wait.'

He swung Clay round and dug in his spurs. The firing was becoming more sporadic. He freed the rifle and worked the lever fast, going over the rise of the hill. The sun blinded him.

He blinked and purple lights gleamed on the inside of his eyelids.

The Cheyenne were charging in on the sod house, firing as they came. Hart noted bows and rifles being used more or less equally. Saw the smoke of replying fire from the windows. Two guns at most.

He held the rifle in his right hand, resting it across Clay's neck and firing twice. The shots went harmlessly over the Indians' heads but diverted those nearest to him; three of them wheeled towards him. Hart ducked low and pushed the barrel of the rifle under the horse's neck, leaning alongside and presenting as little target as possible. He kept Clay between himself and the Cheyenne, dropping one of them with a snap shot which caught him high in the chest and sent him spinning from his pony's back.

The other Indians were peeling away to the left side of the house. Hart began to haul in on the reins, freeing his left boot from the stirrup. As the door came close he jumped and ran, keeping his balance. The door was thrown open and Hart ducked inside, hearing it slammed to behind him.

They looked at him: man and wife, one son. Hart's eyes searched for the second. He was stretched out on the floor close by the far wall, arms crossed over his chest, eyes shut. His hands were strangely white against the dark material of his shirt; the skin of his face grey. A red wound gaped in the lower part of his stomach. Over his heart someone had set the family bible.

'Here they come!'

The man called the warning and pushed the long barrel of the Sharps through the glassless window.

Hart hurried across to the other window, the boy making way for him. He waited until the Cheyenne were well within range and began firing rapidly, accurately. Three braves fell before any of the Indians were inside fifty yards of the house. The Sharps dealt with another.

The leading Cheyenne threw up his arm, holding his war club aloft and shouting at the others to turn away. Hart sighted the Henry and shot the Indian through the centre of the forehead: one second the face was there, painted with white and yellow stripes, mouth open, the next it had all but disappeared in a welter of blood and flying bone.

An arrow thudded into the tightly packed sods close by the window; a few more shots came from the retreating braves.

Two riderless ponies stood close together, blankets draped across their backs, rawhide reins hanging to the ground. Apart from the Indian Hart had just shot, three other braves lay on the ground in front of the house.

'D'you think they'll come back?'

Hart looked round. The father was standing up, reloading the Sharps. 'Depends,' he answered, looking back through the open window. 'How mad they are. How drunk they are.'

Hart looked at the family. The father stood close by the other window, leaning on his Sharps. A bloody streak ran along the top of his balding head; more blood darkened his left sleeve, seeping through his shirt and the heavy wool of his coat. His thin body seemed tired, almost fragile – close to breaking.

His wife was sitting down, bending forward over the table, head towards her hands. Her hair had come unfastened and sprawled, long and greying, all about her face. The veins on her arms were more pronounced than before, like thin, dark snakes wound about her skin.

The surviving son was around fifteen. An arrow had caught him in the shoulder and his father had leaped to pull it out. Now the wound needed dressing and every fresh movement caused the blood to run freely. He looked back at Hart with a show of braveness, but there was no mistaking the fear which lay close behind.

The woman lifted up her head and used both hands to move her hair back. She opened her mouth in a wordless sigh.

'We was down to the last of our shells,' said the man. 'If you hadn't happened by we should never have held out.'

'I saw the little girl,' said Hart.

The man's face clouded. 'Before that last raid . . . we sent her out. Told her to run an' keep runnin'. We didn't want them savages to get her.'

He closed his eyes at the thought, wracked by the images it threw up.

The woman raised both arms. 'My God, I pray it's over!'

'Amen, mother.' The man came towards her. 'Amen to that.'

The sound of pony hoofs punctuated the end of his sentence.

Hart knelt down beside the window frame and checked the load on the Henry. 'When that Sharps runs out, I'll pass across my rifle an' use the Colt.'

They were coming in fast, split into two groups, half a dozen in each. Most of them fired from horseback as they rode, though at that range and speed only luck was going to count. Hart levelled the Henry and waited. Beside him the boy stared through the window, an old pistol unsteady in his hand; he had three shells left.

Just as the Cheyenne came within striking distance something blurred at the edge of Hart's vision. Something moving into it from the left. The boy had spotted her first.

'Amy!' he shouted. 'It's Amy!'

He jumped up and stared at the running, stumbling figure of the little girl as she careered along in the path of the oncoming Indians.

A bullet hammered into his chest, shattering several ribs, breaking the breast bone apart. His body was rocked backwards by the impact and as he went back his legs began to give way beneath him. The pistol fell from his hand and struck the floor. The boy's eyes were closing as he sank down to his knees; his hands pulled at his shirt and were already sticky with blood.

'Joseph!' The mother's wail of anguish cleaved the room.

Hart fired the rifle twice, aiming into the centre of the right-hand group, then shouted at the father, who was on his way to the door.

'Stay here!'

He pushed the Henry into the man's hands and dashed outside. Amy was still coming towards the house and when she saw Hart come out she hesitated, stopped. Two braves were bearing down fast upon her. More were swerving round from the other side.

Hart ducked and went for his Colt. An arrow sped over him with a clear thrum and Hart thumbed back the hammer and fired. The Cheyenne toppled from the back of his piebald pony and bounced on the hard ground. The second brave reached a wiry arm down towards the terrified girl. Hart shot and missed. The hand grasped her dress, hauling her up. Hart held his breath and fired again: so little margin for error.

The slug drove into the Indian's neck immediately below the jawline at the left side, bursting it wide. Amy fell past the pony's legs.

Hart could hear the sound of his rifle being fired from the house. Cheyenne galloped around him. He bent down and picked up the girl, holding her under his left arm, hard against his side.

He started to run for the door and realized that he was being chased. Turned and saw the flash of the axe blade as it swung across the morning sun. He thrust up his right hand fast, fingers circling the Indian's wrist, holding then pulling. The Cheyenne hurtled from his pony's back and Hart dropped the child, grappling with the brave as they fell to the ground and rolled over and over. The war axe was still in the Cheyenne's hand. Hart kicked up and sank his boot into the brave's stomach. As the Indian went backwards Hart sprang, head driving low into his belly. The axe flew wide.

Hart punched at the Cheyenne's face and felt his knuckles strike bone. He stood clear and reached down inside his shirt. Recovering, the brave saw the glint of the knife blade and tried to leap for Hart's arm.

Hart saw him coming and sidestepped, elbow anchored

against his hip, blade upwards, forearm outstretched. The point forced its way between the Indian's ribs, the weight of his diving body pushing down on the blade so that it sank in almost to the hilt.

Hart grasped his shoulder and held fast, twisting the knife. The Cheyenne's tongue, purple and twisted, lanced out of his mouth; Hart was showered in vomited blood. He pulled the blade clear and threw the Indian aside.

The Henry was still being fired from the house; the remainder of the attackers were falling back. The little girl was a few yards from where Hart had dropped her. He picked her up again and hurried into the house.

Mother and child clung to one another in fervent joy and terror. The head of one son lay close by the feet of the other. Hart and the father looked at one another and there was nothing to say – nothing that would stand saying.

Less than an hour later, Hart was on his way. Two mounds of freshly dug earth stood up from the land beside the sod house and, beside them, a tall, bent man leaned heavily on the long handle of his spade.

Fort Reno stood on the bank of the North Fork of the Canadian River on the eastern edge of the Cheyenne and Arapaho Reservation. Like most military installations of any significance it was more than a basic structure with a surrounding stockade. A number of buildings were gathered together in no particular design – barracks and officers' quarters, a trader's store, guardhouse, bathhouse, mess hall. The frame buildings were reinforced against the possibility of attack and some had internal stockades around them – notably the store. Close by the officers' quarters was the office of the Cheyenne and Arapaho Agency.

Hart was challenged by two troopers as he came close to the army buildings, but apart from that entry and exit seemed easy. A number of places had sprung up around the perimeter of the Fort itself, mostly hoping to make profit from the soldiers. There were more civilians in sight than military, and the army's presence seemed only token. To have placed itself in the law-enforcing role that Fredericks apparently wanted would have been impossible as things stood. Bringing in more men would mean that the government would be seen to renounce its agreement with the Indian tribes. It would also mark a move on the path to giving the Territory statehood.

But an ambitious man might think little of trying to move governments, to raise armies – by whatever means.

Hart tied his horse to the hitching rail outside the Indian Agency, watched by a suspicious Arapaho squatting against the wall. Dusk made everything indistinct. A lantern hung from a hook above the agent's desk. Papers littered it. The agent himself sat back, chair resting on its hind legs, one boot on the edge of the desk.

Probert glanced up when Hart came in, tiredness creasing his face. 'What the hell do you want?'

'You know about an Indian attack on some sodbusters north of here – towards the Fredericks spread?'

Probert closed his eyes for an instant, pinching the skin at the top of his nose between finger and thumb. Then he threw a pen down on to the table and looked at the ink spattered pages. 'I didn't hear no answer. Just another damned question.'

Hart stuck his thumbs down into his gun belt. 'That's right. An' you'll hear it again. What about this raid?'

Probert pursed his lips together and let out a slow whistle. He grimaced as he moved his leg away from the desk and lowered the front legs of the chair to the floor. A draft made the flame in the lantern flicker up the sides of the glass.

'When I saw you at Fredericks' place I tagged you for a nosy bastard an' it looks like I was right. What are these damn sodbusters to you?'

'I saw 'em when they had two boys alive. That was before they got attacked by a bunch of Cheyenne.'

'You sure they was Cheyenne?'

'I know a Cheyenne when I see one. Specially when they're wavin' new Winchesters.'

The agent's chair squeaked sharply. He stared at Hart but said nothing.

'You know any reason why they might be rampagin' round like that?'

Probert drummed his fingers silently on his thigh, thinking. 'Could be. Trail herd came up through here the last day or so. Lazy J. They didn't take to payin' the Cheyenne no grazin' rights, agreed or not. Wouldn't give 'em nothing. Not a steer, not a sack of flour, not a bag of sugar. When the Cheyenne argued, the Lazy J started pullin' guns. Couple of 'em got shot.'

Thoughts chased angrily round Hart's brain. 'Pity you weren't around to do their bargainin' for 'em.'

'I was fifty miles west of here.'

'I bet you were.'

Probert shifted awkwardly in his seat. 'What the hell d'you mean by that?'

'What d'you think I mean? I reckon you knew what was goin' to happen an' you kept well clear just so's it could blow up the way it did. I reckon Fredericks has been prayin' for this to happen an' he didn't want you stoppin' it. You're greedy, Probert, greedy as he is. You double-cross these Indians behind their back making deals with Fredericks about grazin' rights. You let trouble break out when you could stop it. And . . .' Hart stared at the agent hard and long. 'And that ain't all.'

The kerosene lamp bubbled; at the top of the glass smoke had blacked it in thick streaks. It wasn't quite clear in his mind, not yet, but almost. He went and stood alongside the agent's desk.

'How long they been gettin' guns? New guns?'

Probert didn't want to answer. He pushed at the pile of papers on his desk, cleared his throat into the back of his hand, pushed a hand through one side of his thinning hair. Looked again at the dark forming outside the window. When he looked back at Hart, the same pair of faded blue eyes were still staring at him, fixing him.

'You know the trouble with this job?'

Hart didn't budge; didn't answer. Probert slid both hands under the sheaves of papers and lifted them into the air, letting them slide and fall and float back down to the desk top and floor.

'Every damn thing you do, every thing you want, there's

someone back east who says you've got to fill in some fuckin' form in triplicate. Time you've mailed it off an' some fool committee of retired senators and army majors has jawed about it, it's too damn late.

'Government's stuck the tribes on this land and thinks it can forget about 'em. Give 'em as little as possible and maybe they'll act nice and peaceful till they fade away. Well, the Indian ain't like that, an' nor is the white man. While there's land here he's goin' to ride in an' take it. Why shouldn't he? He's done it every other damn place on the frontier. We've done it.'

Hart looked at the tired eyes in the aging face. 'Okay, so you've got a tough job. A shitty job. Maybe one that can't be done. Now give me an answer.'

Probert let the chair down with a bang and stood up. His belly pushed against the material of his shirt. On his belt the marks showed clear where the buckle had been set before the thanklessness of the job had weighted him down.

He went by the window and looked out; he could see Hart's reflection in the glass, watching him.

'Began in the summer. Not too obvious at first. Rifle here, six-gun there. But Indians are like kids with new toys. They can't keep something like that to themselves, out of sight.'

He pivoted round. 'Last month or so supplies've been stepping up. Whisky too. Braves've been riding off the reservation, runnin' off cattle, stock. Maybe raiding settlers – I ain't sure.'

'The army know?'

Probert shrugged. 'Things aren't out of hand. Not yet. They don't want to bring a new troop in here unless there's no other way for it.'

'But if they do?'

Probert fixed a button on his shirt. 'Could mean they write off the treaty with the Cheyenne. Once that happens the whole territory's up for grabs.'

Hart took a pace towards him. 'How long have you known it's Fredericks?'

Probert glanced at him quickly, head angled to one side. 'Do I know that?'

'Less'n you're a fool.'

'So maybe I'm a fool. I know one thing.'

'What's that?'

'I'm past fifty and I ain't goin' to get another job.'

The blue eyes narrowed. 'I knew an old man could've given you ten years or more. Indians skewered him to a chair like he was so much meat. He ain't workin' neither.'

Probert walked heavily back behind his desk and sat down. 'You got proof about Fredericks?'

At the door Hart turned: 'No. But maybe I don't need it.'

Long after the door had shut behind Hart, Pete Probert sat staring at the jumble of papers that surrounded him, seeing nothing.

Thirteen

The dog ran at the dapple-grey mare, barking noisily. A dozen feet off it stopped and braced its forelegs, leaning back on its haunches. Ears back, it growled and rolled its head from side to side. Hart looked at the brown and white mongrel and wondered what was making it mad; if it was incensed enough to make a leap at Clay.

But as the horse came up to it, the growling ceased and in its place the dog gave a high whining sound, long nose lifted into the air.

Hart rode past the animal and on into the stage station. Bigger than Buffalo Springs, Baker's boasted a dozen houses, mostly sod construction. The stage building was made of split logs chinked in with a mixture of sand, mud and lime. It stood, square and solid, in the centre of the station.

Hart headed towards it, noting the half-breed leaning back

against a place with a doorway and no door; a grizzled man in a torn plaid coat who stood opposite fixing the harness of an old wagon. When he glanced behind the mongrel was still following him.

There were three other horses tied up outside the stage company building and Hart's eyes drifted along the brands, checking for Lazy J or any C Circle who might still be around. There were none.

He could see the heads of seven or eight more horses in the corral past the building.

Hart looped Clay's reins round the rail and walked inside. A one-armed man sat on a high stool behind a bar to the right; he looked up and nodded hello as Hart came through the doorway. Three men were sitting round a table midway along to the left. A three-parts empty bottle stood between them, together with three glasses. All the men turned to stare at Hart as he went to the bar.

They saw the flat-crowned hat angled slightly on his head, a leather vest over his dark wool shirt; most of all they saw the pearl-handled Colt .45 tied down in the holster at his right thigh.

'Beer.'

The voice was clear and flat. As the one-armed man got down from his stool the other three looked away. It didn't do to show too much interest in someone who wore a gun like that. Especially not in Indian Territory.

The glass of beer was poured out with little apparent difficulty and slid across the bar. Hart took it and drained half at a swallow. Two more gulps accounted for the rest.

'Let's have another.'

'Sure.'

Hart dropped a dollar piece on to the counter; the man gave Hart his beer and change.

'Thanks.'

'Been ridin' long?'

'Long enough.'

'Warmer today, wouldn't you say?'

'Uh-huh, that's what I'd say – if I had nothin' better to do.'

The one-armed man chose to ignore Hart's sarcasm. 'Come far?'

'Fort Reno.'

'Where you headed?'

'Turkey Creek way.'

'You ain't . . .'

Hart set down the glass with a bang which caused the three behind to shift in their chairs uneasily. 'Mister, you sure ask a lot of fool questions.'

The man tried a smile. 'Nosy, I guess. Plain interested, maybe.'

Hart scowled and said nothing. He finished his second beer and turned away, leaning back against the bar. The three men at the table took a sudden interest in the bottle before them. Hart watched as the half-breed he'd seen in the street came to the door and stood there, staring in.

'What the hell you want, Tacos?' called the man behind the bar.

But Tacos said nothing and continued to stare at Hart.

Hart moved his right hand slowly, thumbing the leather thong away from the hammer of his Colt.

'You want me?'

The half-breed nodded, dark eyes bright. His work pants were patched and patched again; the coat he was wearing was too small for him and his bare arms stuck through the ends of the sleeves not far below the elbows.

'How d'you know it's me you want?'

Tacos licked his lips. 'Tall man with blue eyes and pearl-handle gun. Rides grey horse.'

'What is it?'

'Message.'

'Go ahead.'

The breed's eyes flickered. 'No. You come outside.'

Hart shook his head. 'Say your piece from there.'

Tacos glanced at the one-armed man behind the bar and the three sitting to Hart's right. The brown and white mongrel came slowly up behind the breed and rubbed itself against his leg. Tacos kicked out at it suddenly and the dog jumped back, whining.

'A man, he spoke of killing you.'

Hart held his breath; behind him a chair scraped on the boards. Tacos began to back away from the doorway, nodding his head.

'You come,' he said. 'I will tell you.'

Hart turned towards the bar and looked at the one-armed man, who shifted his gaze away.

'Whisky.'

The man pulled out the stopper with his teeth and when he poured the measure, some of it splashed on to the counter. Hart drank it in a single swallow, then tried his pistol in its holster, checking the ease of movement. He pushed the glass back across the bar and went towards the door.

The light was cold and bright. The half-breed stood thirty feet back from the stage building, waiting, lank black hair shielding part of his face. Further off, to the left, the mongrel dog lay on the ground, forepaws stretched out underneath its long head.

No one, nothing else moved.

Hart took a pace away from the door.

Instinct threw him forwards a second before the sound of the shot. A shell screamed off the woodwork behind where he'd been standing. A second report, a second ricochet. Hart came out of a fast rolling movement with the Colt tight in his right hand, hammer back. He was crouched low, feet spread for balance. The shots had come from a building off to the side. He waited, mouth slightly open, eyes keen as a hawk, every muscle of his body tensed.

He saw the glint of gun metal before the whole of the barrel pushed over the window frame; saw it and fired a foot above. There was a muffled cry and the sound of someone falling.

Hart straightened up a little and waited again.

Watched.

The breed hadn't moved. He was staring at the sod shack also, eyes dark with fear. Several others had come running and now stood on the periphery. Two women with shawls pulled over their shoulders; the one-armed man from the bar; a handful of men, one with a rifle held across his body. Three children, two boys and a girl, all in bare feet and patched clothes, all holding hands. The girl had her hair tied into tight plaits which were fastened with blue ribbon and curved out from either side of her head.

The dog was slowly retreating, growling low in its throat.

Hart's fingers had not moved from the trigger and hammer of his gun. His eyes had not left the building opposite.

The shape of a man became clear beyond the doorway. Merv Griffiths stepped forward, swayed, pushing out his left hand on to the door edge for support. There was a dark, spreading stain low on the left side of his chest and he held his body arched. His pistol was tight in his right hand, but the arm was unsteady.

He came further into the light.

'Your pa should've tied you to the saddle an' whipped you home to Texas.'

The brown moustache moved as Griffiths' mouth grew ugly in a wordless snarl.

'Then again, maybe I should have taken you up at Buffalo Spring.'

Merv Griffiths coughed and his body shook: 'Maybe you couldn't've.'

Hart said nothing, shook his head.

Griffiths came another couple of steps closer and the little girl saw the blood on his shirt and realized what it was. She pulled away from her friends and ran towards one of the women, crying wildly. The boys continued to stare, fascinated.

'Why, boy?'

'Don't call me boy!'

This time he coughed up a sliver of blood and it slid down his chin and on to the front of his shirt like a crimson tear.

'Bein' mad at me weren't enough.'

'You . . . you talked down to me in . . . in front of . . .'

'No, that weren't enough. Who put you up to it?'

Merv Griffiths pressed his left hand hard against the bullet wound in his chest; for a moment his eyes closed and Hart thought he was going to fall, but he recovered.

'Who was it, boy?'

Griffiths began to raise his right arm, the gun still in his hand.

'Don't be a fool. You'll likely die anyway, but if'n you get patched up you might stand a chance.'

The arm came almost level; Griffiths winced as he pressed his thumb down on to the curve of the hammer.

'I seen two boys near as old as you dead for no reason an' laid to earth. Don't make me do it.'

Griffiths opened his mouth and more blood trickled out; his eyelids blinked down and his body swayed from side to side – but the hammer on the gun came back.

In the silence the mongrel's growling rasped inside Hart's brain. He brought his lower lip back tight against his teeth and shot Griffiths through the forehead.

The shell struck dead centre, a couple of inches above the top of the nose. Griffiths was hurled back and his legs kicked out from beneath him as he spun sideways. Soft grey matter from inside the shattered skull flew through the bright, hard air. The exit wound at the rear of the head was large enough to punch through with a fist.

Hart brought back his arm and dropped the Colt down into its holster. He was three paces towards the dead man's body when a fresh gleam of metal caught the corner of his vision. Hart hurled himself sideways, drawing his gun as he rolled over, steadying himself with his left hand flat to the ground. A rifle shell gouged the ground where he had been standing; metal reflected sunlight once again.

Hart fired once, twice; pushed himself to his feet and sprinted across open space. His shoulder sent the door crashing in and he dived in after it. Boots shuffled at the top of the stairs. Hart sent a shot ricocheting off the wall. One slug left.

He darted to the foot of the stairs and took them three at a time. The door at the end of the corridor banged shut. Hart kicked it back against the wall. Frank Peterson was standing by the open window. Before Hart could call out he had dived outwards, head first into space.

The crunching thump echoed deadeningly.

When Hart knelt alongside him, blood was trickling from both corners of Peterson's mouth and his eyes were open, staring at nothing.

'I figured it was your money brought him back,' said Hart. 'What I didn't figure was that you'd be backing him up yourself.'

Frank Peterson blinked and coughed blood on to his shirt front.

'The other thing,' said Hart, bending lower, 'is why? Why?'

Peterson tried to ease himself up on to one arm but fell back again. His face was grainy white except for the twin lines of bright red blood. When he spoke his voice sounded as though it was coming from another body.

'Fredericks, he wanted to buy the ranch. Said he needed the land, the valley. He offered us money . . . a lot of money.' A bubble of blood formed at Peterson's nostrils, then burst. More blood was matting his fair hair, darkening it. 'Carol, she . . . she didn't want to move . . . wanted . . . stay . . . a family . . .'

Hart put his hand behind Peterson's head and lifted it up at an angle.

'Go on.'

'Fredericks sent some men round . . . told me if they didn't get what they . . . they wanted, they'd take it anyway. Kill us. Kill us!'

His eyes lost their focus and Hart shifted his head a little.

'They came once when Carol was in Stillwater. I . . . I sold the ranch . . . the land. When Carol came back and found out, she just left. Right off. I followed her . . . argued with her. In the end she said it. Said about you . . . how she'd met you the once . . . how you were more man than I'd ever be.'

His voice was little more than a whisper and Hart had to bend right over his face to hear what he was saying.

'She . . . said she . . . couldn't love me again . . . not after . . . said I wasn't fit to be . . . father of her . . .'

The sound hissed to silence. Hart shook him, lifted him into a sitting position. 'Where is she, Peterson? Where?'

His head rolled sideways and when Hart moved his hand clear it was damp and sticky with the man's blood. He set him down and stood up. Before doing anything else he reloaded his Colt, the townspeople watching him.

When that was done he walked over towards Merv Griffiths' body; the brown and white dog was alongside him, licking his face. As Hart approached it went back on to its hind legs, growling. Hart bent down and found the gold piece he knew would be there in Griffiths' pants pocket.

'Here,' he tossed the coin to the one-armed man. 'See he gets buried. Write to his father at the C Circle down in Texas. Tell him what happened. Tell it right.'

Hart untied his horse and climbed into the saddle. There was still Fredericks to deal with – now more than ever.

Fourteen

Peters and Chavez were riding along behind the supply wagon; T.C. was sitting up behind the team of two, sacks and barrels and boxes stacked high at his rear.

Hart rode in to meet them, his path due to cross theirs where the trail flattened out after descending a long hill. He came easily, not wanting anything to panic the three men or warn them into flight.

T.C. hauled in on the reins when he saw Hart coming and Chavez raised his arm in greeting. Peters carried on riding, only stopping when he had gone past Hart and turned back round.

'Fredericks has been gettin' pretty mad waitin' for you to show,' said T.C., holding the reins between the three fingers of his left hand.

'He'll see me soon enough.'

'Where you been?' asked Chavez.

'Down the Cheyenne agency.'

Chavez moved his horse. 'Family of sodbusters got . . .'

'I know,' interrupted Hart, his voice tight and hard. 'I seen 'em.' He looked from one man to another, finally letting his gaze rest on Peters. 'They was shot up with brand-new Winchesters. Whisky an' guns.'

Peters held his stare for a few moments, then turned his head aside and hawked up spit from the back of his throat.

'You wouldn't know anything about that?'

T.C. and Chavez exchanged nervous glances: Peters spat at the ground.

'Weren't just odd families. Small place called Stillwater, east of here, whole town got wiped out. Women and kids, too.'

T.C. and Chavez glanced at one another again. Peters let his horse turn through a half circle. There were two to Hart's left, one to his right. He thought T.C. might stay out of it, but couldn't be sure.

'I'm pretty damned sure it's Fredericks supplyin' arms. Only . . .' His voice slowed. '. . . I don't reckon he's carting rifles down to the Cheyenne himself. Which means someone else is doin' it for him.'

Hart looked from one to another.

'Wouldn't you say?'

Peters pulled at his greasy stetson, taking it off and wiping his gloved hand round the inside of the crown. 'You go talk to Fredericks about it.'

'I will. But I'm takin' account of you boys first.'

'What does that mean?'

'It means I'd like my feelin's made a little more definite. About the movin' of these arms, that is.'

One of the wagon horses lifted its head and snickered, shifting to one side. T.C. called to it to settle down.

Peters let his own mount move again; now he was sideways on to Hart and less than a dozen feet away.

'I told you,' he said, 'you go talk to Fredericks.'

Hart faced him. 'And I told you that I want an answer.'

Peters mouth moved inside the drooping moustache. Hart knew none of them was about to talk without a little persuasion.

He leaned back in the saddle and without warning his right hand blurred with speed. The next thing Peters realized was that he was staring down the barrel of a Colt .45.

'Talk!'

'Go to hell!'

Hart worked the hammer.

'You ain't goin' to use that. An' I'm not goin' for no gun.'

A smile edged on to Hart's face. 'An' you're not talkin' either?'

'That's right.'

Hart squeezed the trigger and Peters rocked backwards, clutching his right shoulder where the shell had torn through the skin and a good inch of flesh. His face went white; blood ran over and between his fingers.

'Jesus Christ!' exclaimed T.C. softly, shaking his head in astonishment.

Chavez stared from under his sombrero, thinking how fast he could get his knife from its sheath and hope to throw it.

'Now talk!'

Peters shook his head slowly, mouth shut tight.

Hart thumbed back the hammer and the triple click was loud in Peters' head.

'The next one's goin' to break that arm.'

Sweat ran down Peters' face.

'Tell him,' said T.C. 'For God's sake tell him.'

Peters told him. They'd been making deliveries to the Indians for several months – rifles, ammunition, a few handguns, lately bottles of whisky. Fredericks hadn't helped with the deliveries but he had talked with some of the chiefs. He'd told them the more whites that were enabled to settle, the faster the Indians would lose the last of the lands ceded to them. Fight back, he'd advised them. Fight for what's yours.

And all the while he waited for the Cheyenne to go so far that the government would be forced to act – and when they did, Fredericks would take what he thought was his.

Peters finished talking and it was quiet. Hart released the hammer on the Colt and slipped the gun back into the holster.

'What you aimin' to do?' asked T.C. after a few moments.

'I'm goin' in to see Fredericks. Right now.'

'And us?'

Hart looked at him. 'That's up to you. But if you get in the way, or do anything to stop me, you're dead.'

T.C. swallowed hard and nodded. Hart touched Clay's sides with his spurs and set off north. The Fredericks place was a little over an hour away.

A mile on Peters suddenly lashed his horse into a gallop and rode ahead. Hart lifted the Henry clear, thought, put it back. If he warned Fredericks and he ran, he wasn't going to get far.

Not far enough.

Bonney Fredericks' face was whiter than ever: white as the silk of the blouse she was wearing. She sat astride her horse on a rise to the right of the trail and the sun caught the sheen of her black hair as she inclined her head.

Hart pulled away from the wagon and rode up to meet her.

Close to, her face was strained; fear edged the corners of her dark eyes. There was no make-up on her mouth and her lips were the pale colour of dead skin. She was beautiful like a snake is beautiful: and cold.

She stared at Hart until he was forced to blink and look away.

'You're going to kill my husband, aren't you?'

Then he looked at her. 'Yes.'

'Because of selling guns to the Indians?'

'Partly.'

'Because he tried to make a fool of you?'

'Partly that, too.'

'Why else?'

'I don't know.'

Her fingers round the reins were tight and the knuckles white against the dark brown of the leather.

'But you'll kill him anyway?'

'Yes.'

'Whatever I say?'

'Yes.'

Hart started to turn his horse away but she came after him,

closing the distance between them. Her hand on his wrist was like glass.

'There's a lot of money, I expect you know that.'

'I don't want the money, only what's due to me.'

She raised her eyebrows. 'You're an honest killer.'

Hart looked away and the ends of her nails pressed hard and brittle against his skin.

'When it's done, take me with you.'

For a few moments he didn't react, didn't answer. The pressure on his wrist increased. He looked at her pale face, at the slight rise and fall of her breasts beneath the silk of her blouse, at the intensity of her eyes.

He shook his head. 'No.'

The nails bit into his flesh and when he pulled his arm away there were spots of blood on the broken surface of his skin.

'No.'

He wheeled the grey round and clicked his tongue against the roof of his mouth, touching her with his spurs to bring her into a trot, then a canter. He didn't want to look back and when he did, once, she was sitting in the same position staring after him.

'C'mon.' Hart picked up the pace and tried to clear his mind of anything but Fredericks.

As soon as the place came in sight he slowed the horse again, approaching carefully. There was no sign of the loaded wagon and he guessed that T.C. and Chavez had kept on going, taking the goods with them. There wouldn't have been any point in getting involved any more than they were already.

But Peters . . .

His horse was in the corral, saddle still on its back. There was another horse, saddled, tied up near the front of the house. Maybe Fredericks was planning to make a run for it and something had stopped him, held him up.

Hart got down from the saddle and looped the reins over the corral fence. He lifted the sawn-off shotgun from its holster and automatically checked the load. That in his left hand he flicked off the thong from the Colt hammer and began to walk towards the house.

He saw the movement of the rifle in the upstairs window and stopped dead, drawing his Colt and firing in a fluid movement. Glass shattered and the rifle barrel withdrew. A second shot cracked out in the fading echoes of his own and Hart spun round, facing the barn. He snapped off a covering shot and ran diagonally, heading for the bunkhouse. Another rifle shot followed him as he ducked low and swivelled fast. Peters had come too far round the barn door.

Hart sighted and squeezed down on the trigger.

There was only the right arm to aim at and this time he did smash the bone. Peters fell sideways, almost dropping the rifle but finally clutching on to it. He landed awkwardly and shouted out with pain, rocking on to his back.

Still no further movement from the house.

The rifle hadn't reappeared.

Hart watched as Peters got on to his knees and tried to lift the rifle, but his arm wouldn't function and he knew he couldn't use it with his left hand.

'Throw the gun clear and stand up!'

Peters hesitated, then did as he was told. The metal of the barrel flashed in the sun as it spun through the air. Peters stood up slowly, wincing.

'Get over here.'

He was a dozen feet away from the bunk house when a shot rang out from the upstairs of the house and he stumbled forwards, a bullet low in his back.

Hart fired twice, fast, without hitting anything more than wood and glass.

Peters was face down in the dirt. The fingers of his left hand twitched and formed a claw, pulling on the earth.

Hart reloaded the Colt; the movements of Peters hand ceased.

There was no more movement from inside the house; no more shooting. Hart watched as the blood from Peters' body started to spread across the ground on either side of his chest.

Maybe Fredericks had killed him for giving up – maybe he was at the end of his tether and acting without reason. Perhaps he could see the empire he had schemed and struggled to build up disintegrating before his eyes.

The voice came from the other upper window, edgy and harsh. 'What do you want, Hart? What in hell's name do you want?'

Hart made no reply; waited to see if Fredericks would show enough of himself for it to be worth taking a shot.

'Answer me!'

A few moments later an object was hurled through the window and landed on the ground not too far from Peters' dead body. When it fell, the cord around the top of the leather bag loosened and coins spilled out on to the dirt.

'There's three hundred dollars there. Take it. Take it and go.'

Hart still said nothing.

Minutes passed.

A second bag followed the first and landed with the chink of coins.

'It's you I want, Fredericks. You.'

'There's five hun . . .'

'Come out!'

'I'm never coming out.'

Hart fired once at each of the upstairs windows and sprinted across the open space. Two thirds of the way there a shot gouged the ground close by his feet and he leaped sideways, rolling, firing, running again. He rammed his shoulder against the front door and it held fast. Two bullets cracked through the wood a foot to the left of his head.

He stood back and levelled the shotgun at the lock. The blast ripped the door apart and he dived in, hitting the floor and rolling away to the wall.

Another shot came from the top of the stairs.

Hart fired as he was pushing himself to his feet and heard footsteps running. He went after them, taking the stairs two at a time. Three closed doors.

'Fredericks!'

Hart kicked the nearest door open and jumped through. A wardrobe, a four-poster bed, dressing table with a mirror and countless small bottles and boxes. An ornamented water jug standing inside a bowl.

Nothing else.

'Fredericks!'

Hart moved to the second door and lifted his right leg.

A door opened behind him and the explosion of a gun from close range boomed in his ears. He was already falling when the shell grazed across the top of his back, drawing a line from shoulder blade to shoulder blade.

Hart fired his Colt as he hit the floor and the impact jarred his elbow, sending the shot wide. He saw Fredericks lower the pistol towards him and fired again, snatching at the shot. The slug slammed high into Fredericks' left leg and knocked him back against the door jamb.

The gun fell away from Fredericks' fingers.

He stared at his leg, unbelieving. The entry wound was raw; blood came from it in a steady stream, thick and bright as it ran down his pants leg.

Hart stood straight and thumbed back the hammer on his Colt.

'That's nothing,' he said bitterly. 'Nothing to what you've done.'

'I haven't . . . I've never . . .'

Hart lashed out with his right arm, the sight at the barrel end tearing a bloody line down the side of Fredericks' face. The man went back against the wall and shrieked with pain.

'All that happened was you didn't see. You didn't see the bodies. What happened to them. What was done in your name. So that you could own so much land, so much wealth. Power.'

He came close and Fredericks flinched, turning his head aside.

'Power,' Hart repeated. 'Your money and other people's guns. Well, when you tried to buy mine you bought the wrong one.'

There was a footfall on the stairs.

Bonney Fredericks was three steps from the landing. She stared at her husband's face, at the wound deep into his leg; her face was expressionless, stone, white stone. She glanced at the Colt in Hart's hand then turned away and walked back downstairs.

Fredericks watched her go. His mouth faltered: 'Bonney,' he said. 'Bonney!'

The blood from his leg was running into his boot; he reached down his hand gingerly towards the hole in his leg – his fingers sank through the soft, shattered flesh.

Hart stepped away, keeping the gun level.

'You hired me as your regulator, well . . .'

He turned and went to the top of the stairs and Fredericks' mouth gaped, relief showing in his eyes.

Hart turned fast and fired twice: head and heart.

Fredericks was hurled back against the corner of the wall then bounced towards the stairs, folding over the bannister and swinging like a lifesize doll.

Hart walked down the stairs. Bonney Fredericks was sitting in front of the bookshelves; she made no attempt to look up when Hart went into the room. He left and stepped towards the ruined door. Blood fell from the top of the stairs down on to the floor with a steady splashing sound: dark, red rain.

In the sky the sun was thickening towards dusk and clouds shifted heavily across it. Hart untied his horse. The two bags of money were still on the ground, coins scattered loose. Hart picked them up, pushing them down into his saddle bags. He climbed into the saddle. When he looked back at the house he half thought he might see Bonney Fredericks' pale face at one of the windows: there was nothing.

He pulled at the reins and moved the grey past the corral fence. The graze across his back made him shift uneasily in the saddle and he could feel the shirt sticking to his back with the blood.

He didn't know for sure where he was going except that it had to be away. Dusk gathered about him and within a short while only the sound of his horse's hoofs picked him out. The fall of blood from Fredericks' body had slowed, but not stopped.

John B. Harvey
Hart I: Cherokee Outlet 75p

Wes Hart is *The Regulator*. Ex-soldier, ex-Texas Ranger, ex-rider with Billy the Kid, he's tough, ruthless and slick with a .45. He's for hire now and he isn't cheap.

When a double-crossing gunman called Quint stole Hart's horse from a Stillwater saloon Hart went all out to see his blood spattered all over the Eufaula prairie. Then Quint joined a cattle-rustling set-up under Belle Starr, and Hart was appointed to clean them up real good.

Ed McBain
Guns 80p

Colley Donato loved guns. He was sixteen when he first shot a guy. Brought up in Harlem, amongst the hookers, pimps and junkies, a gun wasn't a luxury, it was a necessity. Folks either liked you or killed you.

On the liquor-store job he killed a cop and wished he hadn't. Being on the run is no joke, even for a pro like Colley. Cops everywhere. He had some help from his friends but in the end it was all down to him. And he knew it.

Dick Francis
Trial Run 95p

Ex-steeplechaser Randall Drew is sent to Moscow to investigate the identity of the mysterious 'Alyosha' who is threatening a royally connected candidate for the Moscow Olympics. The brief is vague, and the opposition invisible . . .

'Great stuff, with Soviet heavies breathing down necks and a KGB pornographic set-up' EVENING STANDARD

Michael Hartmann
Shadow of the Leopard £1.25

'I'll exterminate you and all your seed if it takes me a thousand years!'

Newsman Ben Dryden, assigned to South Africa to report on the Woolf diamond-mining family, needs a good story to save his reputation as a foreign correspondent. With the beautiful heiress Rina McNeil he uncovers a generations-old murder plot and a band of ruthless terrorists intent on removing anyone in their way . . .

'Brutality and betrayal . . . murder, feuds and full-blooded thrills'
YORKSHIRE POST

Richard Ben Sapir
The Far Arena £1.25

Eight metres down in the Arctic ice an oil drill strikes into human flesh – the icebound body of a man nineteen centuries old, suspended between life and death by a freak of metabolic chemistry. Modern medical technology slowly restores to life the body of Lucius Aurelius Eugenianus, greatest of the Imperial gladiators. A tale of gripping complexity unravels the political confrontations of Ancient Rome and the moral dilemmas of a modern world where science has advanced too far for its own good . . .

Frank Ross
The 65th Tape £1.25

It began with a letter from the grave . . . a dying man's confession that could not be publicly revealed. The message: a group of powerful men responsible for the three most cold-blooded assassinations of the century are within sight of putting their candidate in the White House. For Washington Intelligence, there is only one solution – their only weapon that snatch of recorded conversation, a terrifying recital of political murder and top-level corruption.

'One of the most exciting, intricate and clever thrillers of the year'
DAILY MAIL

Kit Thackeray
Counterflood 95p

Death, diamonds and intrigue in the Brazilian jungle – when Kees Kuyter, left a cache of diamonds from the jungle deathbed of an aged prospector, is plunged into a desperate cat-and-mouse chase across the continent. Noelia, his beautiful girlfriend, is dead, the diamonds have gone, and Dr Lani, the unscrupulous surgeon, finds an autopsy strangely profitable. Crooked dealers, paranoiac film stars, and Ginny, the publicity agent whose courage is invaluable, compete in the struggle for survival.

Victor Canning
Birdcage 95p

'A kindly but aimless hero fishes a failed nun out of the sea off Portugal, and at last finds a worthwhile reason for living – and also maybe a pointless reason for dying . . . the ex-nun's inheritance . . . carries possible ruin for her true father and a chance for British Intelligence to restore a long-lost canary to its birdcage' OXFORD MAIL

'Intrigue and blackmail and violence in the steely world of "security" ' SUNDAY TIMES